CHAD

Plateau
du Djado

D E S E R T

Massif de
l' Aïr

Adrar Tamgak

Iferouâne

Assoude

Monts Bagzane

Massif de Taghouaji

Agadez

Bilma

T é n é r é

Grand erg de Bilma

Grand erg

Tanout

Nguigmi

Takiéta Zinder

Kantché

Matameye

Diffa

Daura

Lake
Chad

Hadejia

Komadugu Gana

NIGERIA

CAMEROON

Kano

STILL WATERS IN NIGER

STILL WATERS
IN NIGER

KATHLEEN HILL

TRIQUARTERLY BOOKS
NORTHWESTERN UNIVERSITY PRESS
Evanston, Illinois

TriQuarterly Books
Northwestern University Press
Evanston, Illinois 60208-4210

Portions of this book appeared earlier, in slightly different form, in *Global City
Review, Prairie Schooner,* and *The Kenyon Review.*

Printed in the United States of America

ISBN 0-8101-5089-1

Library of Congress Cataloging-in-Publication Data

Hill, Kathleen.
    Still waters in Niger / Kathleen Hill.
        p. cm.
    ISBN 0-8101-5089-1 (alk. paper)
    I. Title.
    PS3558.I3897S74 1999
    813'.54—dc21   98-55428
                                                            CIP

The paper used in this publication meets the minimum requirements of the American
National Standard for Information Sciences—Permanence of Paper for Printed
Library Materials, ANSI Z39.48-1984.

Map by Cyndy Johnsen

Clifford

Then and Now

Our feet are standing within your gates, O Jerusalem.

— Psalms 122:2

CONTENTS

PROLOGUE

A one-legged boy in gray Bermuda shorts is leaning on an aluminum crutch, his back to the desert. His single foot rests sturdily in a rubber flip-flop. He is standing in the *auto gare* in Zinder, hand stretched in front of him to receive the alms of travelers descending from the *taxi brousses* that jostle in and out all day, coming and going between Matameye, Nguigmi, Maradi, Agadez. He is nine years old, maybe ten, and is wearing a white cotton shirt printed with tiny blue and red flowers. His eyes are teasing, a little languid, those of a child who is not deceived by promises. A promise implies a future, and it looks as if he is concerned with now.

Beside him is a girl of about his own age, but it is difficult to say. She is wearing a yellow dress stitched at the neck with brown thread and is lying on one hip in the sand, her hands curled loosely around the blocks of wood she uses to pull her body, rocking, from here to there. Behind her are the tracks her legs have dragged in the sand, deep gulleys ringed in shadow. She, too, might stretch a hand in front of her, but someone would have to lean way down to leave a coin there or else drop it from a height.

The tip of the boy's hollow aluminum crutch is lodged securely in the hole it has made in the sand. It points toward the center of the earth, has sunk like the shaft of a well, downward. It points beneath the loose sand, beneath the ribbon of compressed sandstone sixty feet wide, to water waiting there in darkness, stored during the Pleistocene when the Sahara

1

was a garden lively with antelope and butterflies. The crutch holds the boy upright. But if, like the girl, he were stretched on the sand, he might lower his head to the murmur of retreating waters. Does he have any recollection of an early morning meadow under dew, of running there on two good legs to greet the sun? Does he ever wake from a dream of pomegranates hanging beside swift-flowing streams? Of cool clear pools drenched in shadow?

Perhaps the girl has her own ripples of memory. Perhaps she likes to make up songs about tadpoles and snails, of wheatfields gathering sun. But whatever her rhymes, she probably sings them only to herself, matches her silence to the boy's. After all, what are they to say to each other of such things?

The boy's black foot, resting in its rubber flip-flop, is streaked white with the dust that sifts everywhere. Dark leather patches are fastened at the girl's knees to protect them from their daylong journey over burning sand. The sky is a white sheet of flame.

Could, then, the place where they are be called the desert?

No, it is the Sahel, the edge of the desert, its fringe. There are struggling millet fields outside Zinder as there are across all of southern Niger and on into Burkina Faso and Mali. Farmers turn the soil, such as it is, with iron-pronged hoes. They watch the sky. They save the best seed from any harvest for next year's planting. This is not a country of sand dunes and scree. Not far from Niamey, giraffes skim at dawn to the banks of the River Niger, where fishermen are already casting their nets.

That is, if it is not a season of drought, if the riverbed has not dried and cracked open, casting up bones and bits of stone and root. This is not what is called the desert and yet the crops may fail, the granaries stand empty. The desert laps at the millet fields, draws back. For centuries, now, and in cycles, there has been drought: the gradual but unmistakable reluctance of the sky to fill with rain clouds, the hopeful plantings, the rueful harvests, the mortars empty at daybreak, the flattened breasts, the crying children, the weary laying of bones in sand. Is it true, what some say, that the slow seep of the desert cannot be stopped? Or is it rather an instance of human neglect, of soil turning to sand for want of care?

Whichever, the paved road running east out of Zinder, past the fort, past the abandoned airport, continues unchecked until, almost 500 kilometers away, it comes to an abrupt stop near the shrinking shores of Lake Chad. There, close to windy white dunes, fishermen who have remained in villages once perched on the edge of the lake now carry their *pirogues* a hard hot distance before lowering them into the water.

From where the children wait in the *auto gare*, they can lift their eyes to the dusty fort on its pile of rocks. The square tower of the fort points straight up, a finger raised to the unblinking sky. But the rocks, perhaps, remind the children of water. These are immense boulders of granite, worn smooth as the shells and flat stones that roll unresisting on the floor of the ocean. Poised lightly in a mound, daylight pouring between, they look as if they have been tossed in warm currents and left to settle in God's own time. Or have broken from below, burst sky high from the dark waters buried beneath the sand. They tip and almost fall, do not. They teeter on the edge. Like the sand on which they float, the rocks are washed in changing light and color: fractured white at noon lapsing to orange and finally the quick purple shadows of night. The children, bound so close to the earth, must wonder at this carefree tumble. What would it be like to leap into the air and take a long long time coming down? To feel the lift of one's heart in one's feet? Perhaps they have wondered in the same way at other spills of rock, scattered here and there around the edges of the city: on the road coming in from the west, or up by the marketplace where camels are sold on Thursdays.

But there is no way they could know that to the traveler approaching Zinder for the first time, passing between the bounding rocks that rise like gates on either side of the road, the rocks seem a warning, an assurance, a promise, that in this part of the world gravity does not always hold.

PART I   ZINDER

Auto gare

My eldest daughter, Zara, and I, up from Matameye together to find the house we lived in seventeen years ago, step off the *taxi brousse* into the burning sand. The sky at noon is white. At this time of day no one who can help it is out in the open, head bare to the sun. People sit with their knees drawn up in front of them in the slender shade of a mud wall, or huddle beneath a straw mat elevated on four sticks.

Certainly seventeen years ago Zara and I would not have been hesitating this way in the full blaze of the sun. She would have been at Mme. Renault's *école maternelle*, taking a drink of water from the blue plastic canteen that hung from her neck or learning the word in French for goat. Scratching the prickly heat on her shoulders, yanking the elastic from her ponytail. I would have been thinking about going to pick her up, wishing we had already eaten our couscous and sliced tomatoes so it would be time to close our eyes on a world too bright to look at: Mike, limbs flung wide in instant sleep, Zara and Lizzy, tossing, whispering, overcome at last, and Tulu, baby round as a pot, fingers twitching, sweat standing on her forehead. Time to wait, undistracted, for the shadows to tip, the sand to cool, the sky to appear in stars. For this day to turn into the next. Time to wait for the children to grow up.

Zara drops a coin in the one-legged boy's palm and then, leaning down, places another in the little girl's. They look at the coins, murmur a thanks, and turn away.

"*An gode Allah.*" Thanks be to Allah.

The *gare* is strewn with waiting taxis, vans whose doors will swing shut when each of their seventeen seats is filled with one passenger or more. Early this morning in Matameye, eighty-seven kilometers away, where Zara is working in a clinic and where I have come from New York City to visit her for a month, we were among the first to take our places. We sat talking back and forth an hour or more, looking up through the window of the van into the spiky branches of a *gawo* tree. This is the rainy season, such as it is, and storks are nesting. We could watch their descent, the long fragile legs pushed forward to break the flight, the feet closing round a branch, the leisurely folding of black wings. They stood on the sides of their nests, beaks opening and closing like shears. By the time the taxi was filled, the sun was hot. Nor did the *gawo* give any shade. During the dry season this tree, in a landscape of sand and thorns, ineffably breaks out in tiny green leaves. But during the rainy season it is dry as a stick.

In Zinder both *gawo* trees and storks are more scarce. Vultures are the preferred bird, vultures and black kites, seen wheeling against the blank face of the sky. Fifty miles north, fifty miles closer to the desert and to a lack of food and flourish.

More scarce, but not less distinct. That last month in Zinder seventeen years ago, when leaving had come to seem unendurable, when each evening had brought to a close one more day to which it would be impossible, ever, to return, there had been a pair of storks. The first rain had still not fallen. It was May, the seeds were in the ground, thirsting. We dragged our beds outside each night to escape the heat and slept on the sand in front of the house, faces raised to an immaculate sky. We could look directly up into the wheel of the heavens and see the stars moving above our heads toward morning. The day began while it was still dark with the name of Allah, with the call to wake and praise Him. By the time we had raised dreamy hands to brush away the first flies, men and women all over Zinder were kneeling on mats, dipping their foreheads to the sand, leaning back on their heels.

It was then the storks began their to and fro, their journeys directly above our heads to the *gawo* tree on the other side of the wall. From our beds we could see the beginnings of the nest at the top of the tree, wisps gathered in a crook between two branches. Above us, the slow flap flap of great black wings, the soft white underbelly, the preposterous beak with its dangling bit of string or straw. The three little girls got up and came to lie on our bed, throwing their arms and legs, sweet from sleep, in our faces. We all lay still, watching the storks build a safe and sturdy place for offspring we would never see.

Here we are, Zara and I, stepping off the *taxi brousse* onto the burning sand. She has dropped two coins: one into the hand of the boy leaning on the crutch and another into the little girl's. They have murmured their thanks and have turned away. We are off to get a drink at the Boissons Fraîches, anything to get out of this sun. We are tramping up the sandy incline to the street that runs through the center of the town. A bush Fulani, a Bororo, is striding down; his head is shaved clean from his forehead up to the crown; in back, a line of delicately woven braids are hanging to his shoulders. "Funky," that's the word Zara uses to describe him. He is wearing a leather skirt and white plastic shoes molded to include eyelets and a tongue. His long bare legs are moving like a fashion model's, bent far back at the knees, his feet are pointing slightly out. He looks straight at Zara, eyes ringed with blue. Around his neck are strings of amulets.

She looks back at him and we pass on, up toward the street, the street on which I wonder if she remembers we once watched, on market days, the long caravan of Tuaregs coming into Zinder from the north, the caravan bringing salt gathered from the pits of Bilma.

But is it possible to become extravagantly attached to a place where you are entirely an onlooker? Where you have no job, no appointment to keep? No letter of introduction, no plan for tomorrow?

An Irish-American woman with very little knowledge of spoken Hausa, seventeen years ago I looked sideways at a world I didn't understand. While the children played in the sand with bits of wood and stone, and Mike gathered material for a dissertation, I sat in a wedge of shade and watched the time pass.

It began with the veranda spilled clean with morning light, the gleaming floor, early, before the day's heat had gotten under way. Ripples of shade on a wall already stroked with light. By mid-morning all that had changed: the shadows ran along the floor in swift black channels, unstoppable. Noon, and there was only an abrupt pool, dark and very still, always in the same place in front of the ledge from which the wooden door had been swung back on its hinges and held against the wall with a stone. For at least an hour the shadows seemed not to move at all while the sun hung at the top of the sky; then, too slowly to be sure when, the pool in front of the open doorway tipped east. Again, the pause, the moment of stillness, before the pull back into darkness. By the time Zara and Lizzy, tired of lying in bed, had hauled Tulu out of her crib and fastened her into the stroller, the rush toward evening had begun. Bare feet flying, they raced her up and down the veranda, weaving through the alternating strips of shadow and sun.

Zinder was a case, always, of unrequited love.

Desire was fed on glimpses and surmises, on bits of knowledge baffled and withdrawn. The wind that blows down across the Sahara during the winter months is the same wind that in France is called the mistral, in Italy the scirocco. From North Africa it sweeps across the desert and on southward to the coast where it funnels into the Bight of Benin, spending itself at last in the Gulf of Guinea. South of the Mediterranean this wind is sometimes called the harmattan and in Zinder fills the air with flying sand so pure that for a time everything is seen through a mist. You could be walking along a stretch of sand. In the distance, a shape, a shadow. At first, it is only that. Then something can be seen bubbling up from the surface of the horizon, a dark tangle rising to a narrow twist, like a cyclone, before erupting anew in some fever of impulse and delight. Where have you seen this before? Surely no place on earth. Then there it is, the great silver baobab, its roots exposed to the air and sky, its trunk flung wide in a spray of leaf and branch.

Or this: a caravan of Tuaregs moves through the center of town, camels emerging one by one, ragged knees adrift. And there, lofty in his saddle, bare feet riding a white swaying neck, is a man in an indigo turban, his mouth covered, his eyes looking down into yours. The caravan passes, it disappears in the yellow air, gone, the sloping back of the last beast moving into obscurity.

In a dream, you see the birds screaming over one dimpled place in the water, then the spray, the jet of mist, followed by the back rising from the deep, the creature emerging from the waves, up, up, until even the great blind face is bared dripping in the sun. The sense of having known it all from the beginning, from the other side of the womb.

Would I have fallen so hard if Zinder at first sight had

appeared less monotonous, less grim? Something more than a windy scrap of sand where the heat made a nightmare of each new day and for relief the eye fell on a twist of thorny branch, a vulture hunched on a wall?

The streets were open stretches of sand, deserted during the long middle hours of the day except for an occasional donkey huddled against a wall for shade. By noon the sky had become a flat dim surface, an expanse of emptiness so dazzling the gaze reeled backward and away. Nor were we strangers to Africa and its sun. Both Zara and Lizzy had been born on the coast of Nigeria, a place where steam rises visibly from a rain-soaked forest and where faces stream with sweat. But this was a different sun. In Zinder it blotted up every drop of moisture as soon as it hit the air: you had to drink, never forget to drink, if you didn't want to become ill with dehydration. Or take salt pills. There was no help for it; the sun absorbed sweat before you could lift a hand to wipe it away. What's more, sand settled in ears and nostrils, lips cracked and bled. At noon flies clustered on the bite of food lifting to your mouth, giant cockroaches scuttled at night. Nor did any of this change. On the contrary, there was more to come: toads in the shower, dysentery, scorpions.

Yet it was on Zinder, floating the seeds of life and death indifferently, that desire fastened. Little by little the outlines of a face emerged, maddening in its elusiveness. Impossible to summon at will, desired beyond reason, it would disappear for days, then swim suddenly into view. Visible at first only from a distance, it fascinated by its air of extreme mystery. But gradually, and much more dangerously, it startled at midday, rising from beneath a swarm of flies. Without the least warning, it would be staring out through the empty sockets of the skull of a goat half-buried in the sand.

It was then you were reminded of the beginnings of passion: the terrible jolt of recognition, the bleak notice that what you had thought commonplace, even undesirable, has become as necessary to you as your breath and that without it you will die.

The lover never has any history, any past: no mother, no father, not to mention husband or wife. Not a single child. Nothing that will serve as identification or credential. Nothing by which anyone can say, "Didn't I see you once, a year ago, in the station waiting for a train?" No, all of that is spurned, rejected. It is the unleashed self, released from time and history, the lover offers in cupped hands. All the rest is an embarrassment, a source of confusion and lies. The child playing alone at twilight, the fifteen-year-old wandering in the rain, only these are of any use from the past. And in some sense, at least, the lover, waiting to be snatched wide and set adrift, is right: any attachment at all would only encumber and restrain, provide an intolerable impediment. The whole point is to stand again on the brink, to return to that moment before choice bound one to a slowly turning wheel of days; to fling oneself once and for all into eternity.

The traveler, rushing blindly to an assignation, is the same. Bag packed, everything left behind, the blaspheming hope is that one can be released from a self mired in history. Gone, the stupid face of the clock, fixed at seventeen minutes after three. Gone, the leaves yellowing on the tree outside the window. This time, if no other, myth will overtake one's own stumbling story and all the griefs and longings spilled so messily over the sad confusion of one's days will at last assume a noble shape, both tragic and anonymous: Orpheus, unable to resist the backward glance. Demeter, crying for her daughter.

The Street

We pause, Zara and I, despite the sun beating on our heads, before leaving the sand for the street. Zara has turned to speak to three older women, Fulanis, who like ourselves have walked up from the *auto gare*. Heads free of the enormous netted bundles they have lowered to their feet, they are nomads taking a moment of rest. Each woman's hair is bunched in poufs at either side of her head and again—although here bare scalp shows through—on top. The rims of their ears are pierced up and down with seven holes, but silver hoops hang from only some of them. One woman lays her hand on her breasts and says that they have traveled from Agadez to visit their children in Zinder. Then, asking a boy standing nearby to help hoist the bundles back onto their heads, each a staggering load, they are gone.

"Fulanis," Zara says, "coming and going."

We see only their backs as they walk in a line up onto the street, legs thin as herons', indigo cloth tightly wrapping their hips. Then we follow them onto the tar.

Zara is my own dear daughter. She has come to Zinder with me today, is walking beside me on this stretch, to help find the house we lived in so long ago, but also to humor my wish. If it were left to her, she would probably let the whole thing go. She has already done her own foraging of the past. And after all, her past is not mine. In Zinder she was six years old. I brushed her hair the color of honey from her neck in the mornings, gathered it in a ponytail, sometimes tied it with a ribbon. I kissed her face, first one cheek, then the other. But what did I know?

"Oh yes," she tells me, "it all came back when I returned two years ago, everything, everything, waking up in the morning to the sound of pounding and roosters crowing, the sky at night. I remembered the rocks outside of Zinder, the corrugated gates scraping against the sand."

But what all this means to her I have no words to ask. The things she might say casually to a stranger about her child-hood—I had this kind of a mother, this kind of a father—she cannot say to me. Again, the words stick in her throat: did you know how hurt I was that time, how afraid? I have only glimpses. A night of suffocating heat when she lay awake until dawn trembling in fear of mosquitoes and malaria; I have heard about that. How she lay there imagining her parents dead and herself alone with two younger sisters she had somehow to get on a plane and back to someone who would take care of them all. No more than a glimpse, but it opens to so much else.

And then there are the moments I know nothing whatever about. Moments when she must have thought, this is not my mother. Not this one.

Every now and then, during the two years she has lived in Matameye, working in the Centre Medical, Zara has made the trip to Zinder: to visit friends who live here and at the same time to buy cornflakes or perhaps a jar of strawberry jam. Occasionally, she has looked for the house. On one visit she found the *gardien* who still sat in front of what used to be the Peace Corps office but which is now, she tells me, a hostel for French volunteers.

I remember it well, the squat cinder-block building, the refrigerator empty except for measles and smallpox serum. And except, now and then, for the ice cream Mike made for the children using tins of evaporated milk and a bottle of vanilla extract. The office was on a road that fed into the long stretch of sand on which we lived and sometimes, before we lay down for the *sieste*, he made the half-mile trip up to the refrigerator, returning at a run through the midday glare, all for the sake of the instant when he could put this treat before us, white and cool and still firm. Or, but not very often, I would take the children there as a means of getting through an afternoon, take them to listen on the office machine to the *Peter and the Wolf* tape we had brought with us, to the cat gliding step by step toward the unwary duck swimming round the pond.

When Zara spoke to the *gardien* who until a few months ago still sat in the same place, just outside the gate, he had said yes, he remembered an American family with three little girls—there had been two who were a little older and then a baby—and when she had told him who she was he had clapped his hands together as if everything was cause for wonder but nothing for surprise. No, he wasn't sure where the house was: maybe somewhere near the hospital? But when he took her to it she had recognized nothing and thought he must have been mistaken.

Zara is wearing a *pagne*, a length of cloth wound tightly round her waist and reaching to her flip-flops. On top, she is wearing a blouse cut from the same material, a wax print bought from the Lebanese cloth merchants here in Zinder, Nabil Edouard et fils. A black leather bag, made by Garba, is hanging from her shoulder. I am carrying one exactly like it, a gift she had waiting for me when I arrived a few days ago to visit her here, a visit I am making alone because Mike is teaching at this time. She has bought these bags on one of her earlier trips to Zinder, along with the box of cornflakes.

Garba is a name I know. It is stamped inside the wallet I have carried with me for years, purchased with Zara looking on, head high as my elbow. Purchased, certainly, on a visit to Garba's atelier, designed, like *Peter and the Wolf,* to fill a long afternoon.

At about four-thirty, the little girls and I would push open the gate of our house onto the broad stretch of sand that ran south past the Peace Corps office and up over a dune where an enormous *gawo* tree marked the site of the Muslim cemetery. But this time we were going in the other direction. We turned left, away from the scavenging goats and sheep and the donkeys trotting past with bags of millet on their backs, and for a moment, before turning quickly left again, looked toward the Catholic mission, half a mile away. The second left brought us up onto Zinder's paved road, the road we are walking now, where the wheels of the stroller turned effortlessly. This road fell back into the sand soon after it reached Takieta, fifty kilometers away, but to us none of that mattered. We were going only a short way, past the Boissons Fraîches, to the old part of town where the corners of the houses rose in minarets, and the doorways, carved above with intertwining loops and parallel lines, opened on cool, darkened anterooms. Inside the doorsteps, waiting neatly in pairs, were brown leather sandals or green ones, tooled with red.

It was here, among the neighborhood mosques and the booths where tailors sat at sewing machines and goldsmiths worked with tiny anvils, hammers, and scales, that Garba had his atelier. An unmarked door in a narrow street. Two or three craftsmen sat crosslegged on the floor with him, barefoot, stretching and smoothing skins on wooden boards, cutting and tooling leather, sewing up seams with narrow strips of leather, their fingers closed on the handle of an awl or a knife. Sometimes they would call out to a boy passing in the street and send him for a calabash of *hura*, the milky millet drink sold everywhere, or maybe a couple of Gauloises. The smell of skins piled against the walls, the shadowy cool of the room, the quiet talk and laughter of the men as they sat working, elegant in loose cotton trousers, all this made the atelier a pleasant place to visit.

We came with an order for sandals.

Garba rose from his place by the door, his embroidered *hula* tidy on his head. Striking his chest lightly with his fist, he questions me on the afternoon, on my health, on the little girls, the *yara*. I questioned him on his work and then on his fatigue, back and forth, the prescribed inquiries followed by the sliding reassurances that the children were well, that Allah be praised for the gift of work, each response ending in a hum in the throat, a low murmur of consolation. Then the small bare foot was placed on a piece of cardboard and Garba traced its outline with a blunt pencil. Afterward, he gave the cardboard to one of the men sitting on the floor who slid it into a corner to wait its day.

By six o'clock in the afternoon the walls of the banco-adobe houses, facing each other across narrow passages of sand, floated in the clarifying light that ends each day. The old men had come out of their rooms and were sitting on straw mats in the long shadows, fingering their prayer beads and talking. Children were rolling hoops made from the metal rims of bicycle wheels or chasing each other in circles or carrying firewood home on their backs. And somewhere nearby the boy in the brown tunic was cleaning the open gutter with a long-handled hoe, trying over and over to scrape it clean.

He was said to be a *mahaukaci,* one not like the others. When he saw us he hopped from foot to foot, grinning, teeth askew in his head. He waved to us until we finally turned the corner into the paved street where the fort, at noon lost in a white blaze of light, hovered dreamily above the town, flushed bronze like the boulders on which it sat.

Inside Zara's black bag is a blue plastic canteen containing iodized water. Each morning in Matameye she squeezes five drops of iodine into a gin bottle filled with water so that I can drink without getting sick. When she first arrived in Matameye, she tells me, she did the same for herself, but now she drinks water straight from the tap. She is at home here. Her Hausa is rapid and idiomatic, and she readily translates what I don't understand. As we walk along, she throws out greetings.

"*Sannu,* Malam," she calls to a blind man sitting on a straw mat by the side of the road, his bowl in front of him. His face is deeply pocked and his eyes have all but disappeared behind straining lids. He murmurs a response and inclines his head thoughtfully, as if listening for more.

A boy is coming toward us through the shimmering heat. His knees, frank beneath the cut of his shorts, are no longer those of a child, and the hands hanging at his sides are large. On his head, drawn down firmly over his ears, is a knitted red woolen hat, flaps hanging below his chin.

"But aren't you too hot in that?" Zara asks, astonished.

"I'm from the bush," he says, explaining, and they both throw back their heads and shout with laughter.

Zara is leading us along the street, directing our path. As for me, my eyes are fastened on the two pairs of white feet in flip-flops, keeping time.

When we last walked down this street together, it was I who carried the canteen of filtered water so that she could have a swallow if she needed one. I would have been pushing the stroller with Tulu sitting in it, plowing it through the sand, and she and Lizzy would have been holding on to either side, kicking along in sandals made by Garba. Or one of them would have taken a turn pushing the stroller and the hand of the other would be lying sweetly in my own.

A walk down this street made a third outing for an empty afternoon, certainly a more frequent choice than *Peter and the Wolf* or Garba's. We might stop at SCOA's for a bottle of orange *sirop* or a bag of toasted biscottes for Tulu to sharpen her new teeth on. We could while away a good half-hour there, wandering up and down between the shelves of tomato paste and *petit pois,* lingering beneath the slowly turning overhead fans. We said *bon soir* to M. Nasser, ready after his *sieste* in a freshly ironed shirt, who was manager not only of SCOA but of the hotel as well. In a curt, deep voice he would be directing young men who were unpacking boxes of jam from Poland, tubes of mayonnaise from Spain.

M. Nasser drove the single Mercedes in town and had a plump daughter, seldom seen at all, who occasionally appeared alone at a far table in the garden of the hotel. Did she have a mother, somewhere, longing for her return? A sister? An aunt? And what could her days have been, the air-conditioned rooms, the rugs on the cement floors, the empty Pepsi bottles collecting on a table? It seemed, always, she must be waiting for something to happen that would release her at last to Beirut and the mountains slipping down to the sea: for her father to decide he'd had enough of this strip of sand, for SCOA to go bankrupt, the Mercedes to fall apart.

For someone to walk into the garden of the hotel and to recognize behind the languid, tired flesh a self standing at attention.

Leaving SCOA, the little girls and I crossed the narrow

ledge of tar to the sand on the other side of the street. We usually had a particular errand in mind, thought up as we went. A little box of La Vache qui Rit, with its six wedges of cheese each wrapped in silver paper, made a reason to return to Michel's, the shop of the French butcher. But we passed the Hotel Central on the way. Almost always, some vehicle or other was parked in front: a Land Rover or a Deux Chevaux, the Sabena van up from Kano. The garden was a pleasant place to sit, neem trees stirring patches of shade where you could rest and drink an icy beer or Pepsi. In the evening the branches were strung with tiny white lights and people sat beneath them talking quietly and eating the *biftek, pommes frites,* and salad that was served every night along with a carafe of red wine. Sitting in a low chair with your hand resting on the cool sand, you could look up through the neem leaves into the starry night and reflect that here you were, alone and yourself, in this place of all others. That your entire past had brought you unsuspecting to this moment of perfect peace.

Travelers of all sorts stopped here: Italian engineers on their way up to the Aïr Mountains to mine deposits of uranium, Swedish photographers making documentaries of the Tuaregs, someone from Oxfam. But all of them, sipping their cool drinks, had one thing in common: the means to pay. Outside the hotel was a different group altogether, the beggars of Zinder. Or those beggars young or strong enough to endure the sun, the wait, the slow coming and going between the *auto gare* and the hotel. There you did not find the three blind old women, led by a child, whose song could be heard early in the morning outside our gate. Or the dwarf, rolling back and forth, face averted, never any place for long.

Passing the gate of the hotel, the children and I were on our way next door, to Michel's. The first time we entered his shop, soon after arriving in Zinder, something happened we could not forget.

We had ordered our meat. Behind the counter, hanging on the wall as in a *boucherie* in Paris, was a blackboard with the names of all the cuts written on it: *saucisson sec, côte porc frais, lapin.* These came down from Paris—along with cheese and butter from Normandy—on the Air France flight to Niamey, then were flown out to Zinder in a plane that brought mail as well, once a week on Fridays. Luxuries, certainly, which could be purchased only as a treat. On this particular afternoon we had asked for our *côtelettes* and had watched Michel place the raw meat on a wooden block. He measured it with his knife, looked up before he cut, black hair falling across his forehead. *"De trop?"* he asked, then sliced two, three times.

Yes, he said in answer to my question, he had been in Zinder a long time, since the end of the *guerre d'Algérie.* Had never returned to Paris, had kept moving south across the desert and come to a stop here. After he had wrapped the meat in a piece of paper and I had paid him, he looked over the counter at Tulu sitting in her stroller, at Lizzy and Zara standing there fingering the edge of the block, and told us to come, he had something to show us.

We followed him to a door that opened onto a sun-baked court surrounded by a low wall. In the doorway he had stopped short.

"Ah non!" he said. From behind his apron, blood-stained and tied in back with string, we could see into a shaded corner where a gray kitten crouched beside a saucer of milk. On the wall opposite, dark against the sun, sat five or six vultures. The butcher had cupped the trembling kitten in his hands and carried it past us inside. Then, on the floor behind the counter, while the kitten lapped the milk, the little girls had squatted next to it and stroked its back.

Before we buy the round of cheese we have to lift the wooden cover of the box and look inside: there he is, six times, the cow laughing with his mouth full of teeth.

Too many days to remember, days cold out of season and days when I would have given my soul for a chill. Days, one after another, so charged with falling light and grainy shadow I took little account of what was nearest of all. So now there's only the remembered press of Zara's hand in mine, now, when it is too late. She is gone, altogether lost, the Zara who walked beside me then, who I might have swept suddenly into a hug, the embrace that might have, oh might have, spared her some sad night, some dim sorrow at noon.

Zara and I are walking through the sand, and she is looking at me, dark eyes alert, asking if this is what I remembered.

I cannot say that the print of her six-year-old hand in mine has left a hollow, a sweet declivity, that does not fill. Her hair, the color of honey still, is brushed straight back and held in place by a folded blue scarf tied at the base of her neck. She tied it on early this morning. She was up before I was, putting iodine in the water, making powdered milk to put on our cornflakes. By the time I was dressed, she had already placed two bowls on the table and a spoon beside each one. The table was covered, as always, with a green cloth, and on the wall above it, facing us as we ate our cornflakes, was a map of Africa with its brave recovered names: Benin, Burkina Faso, Zimbabwe, Zaïre. We drank our coffee from two large plastic turquoise mugs.

The brute fact of it is I recognize nothing. Zinder is a barren place, windswept, so hot I think I better be careful in this sun.

Boisson Fraîches

Did I ever go to the Boissons Fraîches with Zara?

No, I went only once when we were living in Zinder. And that was without her.

In fact, it is no longer the Boissons Fraîches at all, but a little place where you can get a meal. And a Pepsi, as we do now. There are four tables, all empty, and we choose the one that is directly under the fan slowly revolving on the ceiling. When we pull out the chairs to sit down, their metal legs bump and scrape against the cement floor with a sound I remember.

Ahmed comes out, smiling and greeting Zara, whom he recognizes from other times she has come here. He greets me too, the palms of his hands open and at our disposal. This is his place and we are welcome.

His son also calls out a greeting as he carries wooden crates of Pepsi and orange Fanta through the door we have just entered. It is hung with narrow strips of plastic, red, blue, yellow, to keep out the flies. On the wall we are facing is an advertisement for Pepsi: a dripping bottle, cool and dark, riding the air at a slant. *Ça désaltère mieux.* It quenches the thirst, Pepsi, better. Not better than water, certainly, but the water in the blue plastic canteen is warm. It is for the frosty bottle held against the forehead, between the hands, that we have come. And the cold bite at the back of the throat. Next to the picture of the bottle of Pepsi is a poster, handwritten, telling us what we can eat: Zara is going to have an omelette with *pommes frites*. It is too hot to eat, but I am going to have a plate of *petit pois* and onions.

There is a third item on the wall, a formal photograph of Seyni Kountche, the president of Niger. A few days ago, in Matameye, there had been a holiday, as everywhere in the country, to celebrate his return to the presidential palace in Niamey. He is old, unwell, and had remained in Paris for two months following an operation. On the day of the holiday Zara and I had gathered in the late afternoon with the rest of Matameye to celebrate. There had been the drummers in the open field, the women dancing in a line: midwives, prostitutes, *fonctionnaires*. People had run forward to press coins on the foreheads of the dancers as a tribute; after a moment the coins had fallen into the sand. A kind of intoxication, Zara had said, to watch coins—where they are so scarce—glint and fall, unheeded.

While Zara and I eat our lunch, we make a plan. First we will go to the hostel for the French volunteers, rest for an hour so we aren't walking around in the worst heat, then go from there to find our house.

"I've been here before," Zara says. "The day is yours." She pushes the scarf back from her forehead, tucking underneath the hair that has come loose. Then she drops her hands into her lap.

They do what she wants them to do: pour Pepsi into a glass, fix her scarf, hold a fork. The first time I laid eyes on those fingers I was exactly the age she is now: twenty-three. They had to be folded open then, flattened wide. Fists giving way to scaly palms, moist still from their long immersion. Skin that didn't bear thinking of. They lift onto the table when Ahmed's son comes to take our plates away and to ask if we would like anything else. He is wearing a long-sleeved shirt, white, rolled up to his elbows; his arms are black and very thin. His fingers reach for the edge of our plates, grasp and remove. Once coiled tight as snails, flesh unfurled. Another Pepsi, yes. We'll rest here a minute before moving out into the sun.

It is here, sitting under the fan with Zara, that the memory of the fever returns: or maybe even something of the fever itself. The chill seventeen years ago running along the shoulders into the scalp. The blood beating in the face. The bed is low, almost on the floor, a Hausa bed, strips of wood stacked, layered, and bound at the ends with leather cord: the arm flung over the side ends in a hand pressed flat against the cool cement. Cool, but split apart by some swelling from beneath, cracked open to let the darkness out. The raised hand comes up gritty with sand. Opposite the bed is a door, a flat wash of light that plays on the shoulders of whoever is standing in it. The stern glare of noon that, when I close my eyes, makes a white oblong framed in black.

On the other side of the door are the shadows I can't see: pools you could swim in, depthless. On the veranda, periwinkle in a line of red clay pots. At night the white petals fold tight, but during the day they spread above the burning sand like a cloud. I see them in the shadows, cool banks of clover, meadowsweet drenched with dew. And water lilies, some submerged, some open on the air, but all rising, swimming into view. The walls inside the room, left and right, open in arches to rooms just like it.

But high in the corners, dust storms have left their swirling traces on the whitewash, waves of sand breaking dark and tireless against the ceiling.

The child Zara is standing in the door, her face in shadow.

She is standing on the ledge that makes a step between the room and the veranda outside. I look up from the bed and see her short dress, the length of her skinny legs. There are the knees, and above, pointing east and west, the elbows, cradled in her hands. And on top the discrete head. Here she is, dim darling. She steps down from the ledge and walks toward me. I see her take the step down, elbows riding at her sides, face moving into the light. Her knees float forward, endless, like the camel's; they swing loose, first one shin then the other. I am waiting to touch her hand. When she is almost next to me her knees lock in place, a standstill. What has she seen to make her stop? to make her afraid? to make her remember?

Night after night the coughing that madly bruised a spot on my ribs. Beyond the wooden door gusts of wind lift the sand and hurl it in every direction. It hits the shutters with a hissing sound like rain. The weave of the straw mats is glossy beneath Mike's feet as he fills the glass from the clay water-pots standing in their iron tripods. In the room on one side, Tulu sprawls in her crib where each morning the stealthy chicken lays her egg. In the other room, Lizzy and Zara are stretched side by side on Hausa beds, tucked in beneath white nets suspended from the ceiling by hooks. Do they lie awake listening? Do they put pillows over their heads? In the morning the rim of the glass on the floor beside the bed is black with flies.

Again, the old question: why here? And then, in a whisper: I am afraid for my life.

The mother who cannot manage, who cannot do what has to be done. The children are pressing at the door, wanting to come in. No, she is not home. Go away, children, there's no one here.

Here is the mother. She is sitting with a child in her lap. The child puts her head between her mother's breasts. She settles more deeply, breathes and sighs. That beloved shelter, that swoon of content.

The child is standing at the door, looking in. She is holding her elbows in her hands. But what can she do? She is waiting, not knowing what for. In another minute, surely something else. Come, my own. Come so that I can hold you close. Let me stroke your cheek, kiss your knuckles, one by one. If you sit here on my lap, I shall ask for nothing more.

Sickness is one thing, but suppose the mother is perfectly well. Suppose she rises from her bed and sets the house in order. Or suppose she does not. Suppose she sits in a chair and is not sure where things go, what drawer they belong in. Suppose when the children appear in the door, she is not sure which is which, she becomes confused, unable to speak.

In her house in Matameye, Zara has made a room for me. She has fixed a room that was used to store stray boxes so that I can sleep there. In the room there is a brass bed, a straw mat on the floor, and a footlocker where I can put my things away, safe from the sand. On the wall above the bed Zara has tacked up two postcards: a Fulani swinging along with the easy stride of a nomad; the other, one of Van Gogh's sowers, caught in the same languid fling from the hip. There is a piece of netting nailed up around the window. There is also a table covered with a piece of cloth. On the table is an open calabash, waiting to catch a comb, a safety pin, a letter.

The first time I saw the room Zara was making the bed. She had come down to Kano to meet me, where we had stayed with our friend Aïssa overnight, and had left the shutters of her house closed tight against the sand. Wait outside, she'd said, the afternoon we returned, and had gone in to swing open the shutters. I stood with my back to the door and looked around her compound, at the neem trees green against the mud wall, the sand swept into moons, at a lizard with an orange head rigid in the sun. Back in Africa after so many years, spot in all the world where I was young. Zara's first nesting place, refuge of my own first flight.

When Zara called, I turned and stood in the doorway. She was bent over, tucking a sheet fast at a corner of my bed. "The sand," she said. "I left this until we came back."

The sheets were yellow ones my mother had taken off the shelf—my mother, dead these last six months—and given to Zara before she went away. Sheets from a cupboard I once fled to, a child in tears. The smell in the sheets my mother's smell, the sweetness of her arms, oh where and how to remember.

It is much too hot in the sun. The arrow that flies by day. Beneath the sand bones are strewn in every direction. Bones clean as a whistle, dry as grass. These bones are shameless. A wind, and they rise to the surface like a whale rising from the deep. Without a thought in the world. Up, up, and there they are, bathed in the clean light of the sun, careless, tossing aside the sand that streams from their blind and perfect stare.

Ahmed gives us a little piece of paper with the amount we owe him written on it. Four hundred and fifty C.F.A., counted out in bills and coin. He opens cupped hands to receive it; to clutch would be rude. We thank him, and he wishes us a good afternoon. He greets us until the next time. His son does the same. We dip our heads between the strips of plastic and are out on the street again. Done.

The Fort

It must be one o'clock by now, but the sun hasn't moved from its place in the sky. We could be ducking back out into a blizzard where travelers who don't know any better lose their way and perish. Fall down in a swoon and never get up. Today we have a place to go. We are on our way to the hostel.

But suppose we didn't. What then? For how much longer could we have sat at Ahmed's? Another half-hour? The rest of the afternoon? After a time Ahmed would want to close up, shut the door over the colored strips of plastic and say his prayers. What would he have said to these two women sitting in his restaurant? "All I have is at your disposal but not now. Later on, when it is cooler." We would have paid our bill and left, but instead of walking in the direction of the hostel, we would be standing still, staring up at the sky. Watching the black kites and vultures ride a hot high wind and wondering what to do. We might have considered joining a group sitting in the shade of a mat propped up on sticks. We would be welcome. But that would not be a situation it would be easy to continue for long. After a while it would become clear that people's knees and elbows were suffering from cramp.

Enough. The moment had come to move on. But where? To SCOA? To the Protestant *librairie?* To the butcher's? All of these are closed from noon until four. Garba's, the same. We could go to the hotel; we have the means to pay. But Zara has already said it doesn't exist anymore. It is now a discotheque and isn't open during the daytime at all: figures of dancing bodies have been painted on the wall outside it. The *auto gare?* But we have just come from the *auto gare.* The church is locked, the mosque is not open to women.

What's left is the sky we are staring into, the sky that shimmers white behind the fixed and burning point of the sun. The sky that moves in a revolving sphere around the birds pinned against it.

And the sand itself.

The way to the hostel is in the face of the fort. From below, it looks as if a light flame is running along the walls of the square mud tower, burning away the edges. As if the lines of things are being consumed in a blaze of white heat. A flag snaps in the wind, three horizontal stripes, orange, white, and green, an orange sun centered on a field of white. Not even a century old, and the fort is already weightless, like the rocks on which it rests, its uneasy blunt counterforce all gone. There are slits in the walls, once the eyes of the Territoire Militaire narrowed against the glare, alert to meet the unblinking gaze turned in on the fort itself.

The slits look out in four directions.

Half a mile east to the *birni,* the old walled city, where the *sarki,* the sultan, of Damagaram has his palace and where guards in green and red motley, a leather sheaf slung over one shoulder, a bow over the other, still pass in and out, swallows twittering above their heads in the shadowy entrance; where a plaque above the door of a house says that Heinrich Barth stayed there during the month of January 1851.

North to the desert and the flying shadows of Tuaregs, once descending on camels to restore their rule, to Agadez with its ancient mosque, to the oasis nearby at In-Gall, and to the black rocks of the Aïr; north again to the ruins of the Tuareg city of Assoudé, already in decline when the cathedrals of Europe were going up, and—at Iferouane—to the rock paintings of giraffes roaming a grassy plain; north across the Algerian border into the Ahaggar mountains, straight across the Sahara all the way to Biskra, and so at last to Algiers, perched on a sun-coined sea.

And south to Nigeria, to the fourteen-gated city of Kano with its crumbling twelfth-century walls; Kano, city of mosques and minarets, of sun spilling at dusk red across terraced roofs, of plucked music in the night, of the new moon rising to end the fast.

East, north, south: all remain much as they were seventy years ago. But the trading part of town where we are walking now, west of the fort, has languished since the 1920s when the French moved the capital to Niamey, when Zinder was abandoned once and for all as a city dry beyond endurance.

In the long reach of the fort, we see them coming toward us, the one-legged boy and the girl swinging along on her blocks. They move slowly, taking their time. He inches forward, first his crutch, then his foot in its flip-flop. Although he could probably hop nimbly if he wished, he moves no faster than the girl beside him, dragging her legs through the sand. They are talking to each other. Sometimes the boy throws back his head, laughs. One leg of his gray shorts ends just above his knee. The other ends at the point of the stump. The girl places one block in front of her, pulls herself forward, then reaches with the other block. She is barefoot.

When her head is almost level with our knees, Zara greets her. "*Sannu, yarinya,*" she says.

The girl looks up, the tiny gold hoops in her ears glinting in the sun. For a moment she pauses, her hands resting on the blocks. "*Yauwa*," she answers, informal in a child's way, and smiling shows the gap where one of her front teeth is missing.

The boy is leaning on his crutch, arms loose at his sides. He extends an open hand, eyes curious.

This time Zara whoops with surprise and slaps it, laughing. Quick as a flash he turns it over and slaps the palm of hers.

Then they are on their way, brief shadows moving beside them, and we are on ours. But where are they going? Is the stretch between the *auto gare* and what was once the hotel and is now the discotheque still the beggars' thoroughfare? And the plot of burning sand in front of the discotheque, could that be called a place to go?

In Zara's mouth, too, that year in Zinder, the same gap, the six-year-old with the missing tooth.

It was Delisse, one night during the harmattan, who talked about the fort. He stopped by for a drink, stepping through the gate with a flutter of embarrassment disguised as arrogance, raking the blond hair back from his forehead. While gusts of hot wind scattered the sand and lashed the branches of the oleander bush to the ground, we sat on the veranda and talked. Between us, the flames of the candles in their black clay candlesticks from Myrria dipped and straightened. Before he got up to leave, he had told us about the aging parents in the house in Lille where he had grown up, the Aubusson tapestries hanging in the salon, the marble fountain choked with leaves; about his one attempt to return to France and sleep again in beds where the heavy linen sheets embroidered with the family's initials never lost their chill. He had lasted a year, he said, and returned to Zinder to marry a Hausa woman whose father called him "camel eye."

With these words, his face had leapt into view: pale blue eyes, surrounded by faint eyelashes, looking out as if across a distance; the corners of the mouth twitching up in a kind of perpetual grimace that turned into an outright smile when he communicated something particularly painful.

When he first arrived seventeen years before, he told us, the French military presence dominated Zinder. From our house, all the way up to the Catholic mission, the street was lined with bistros to which *maison des filles* were attached. The *militaires* would come down from the fort on the hill to have their *biftek*, their glass of wine, and their *"fille."* As he described the *militaires*, he gestured comically, mimicking their paunched figures and hooded eyes. Then he said simply: "Ah, I have been very disappointed in the French." A moment later: "The European romance with the desert. One can see where it ends. As with so many romances, in the will to possess. And sometimes, you know, to ravish."

Was it true, what he said, that one hundred *militaires* coming down from Agadez in a camel caravan would require a retinue of three hundred women, and that much of the bodily deformity seen everywhere in the town could be attributed to syphilis?

But it didn't begin there, he said, lowering his eyelashes. Before the French arrived, Zinder had been known to do not a bad trade in slaves. Oh yes, we could be sure it was true. His in-laws had told him so. Had we seen the occasional ostrich behind a wall, enormous black and white birds on thick legs? These were leftovers from the 1870s and 1880s, when fashion in all the capitals of Europe had demanded feathers. At that time Zinder had been known for its ostrich farms. Camel caravans equipped in Kano would stop in Zinder long enough to load the feathers before setting out across the desert. At Tripoli they would be taken by ship across the Mediterranean and on to Paris, Berlin, London. And then, bah, fashions had changed. By the 1890s ostrich feathers were no longer wanted and the farms around Zinder had disappeared.

But who did we think had worked these farms, he asked, grinning.

Then he went on to tell us that within living memory there had been three droughts. The worst was in the second decade of the century, when all of Europe was devouring itself in a muddy war. While rain splashed in the trenches of northern France, the sky above the Sahel refused to form a single cloud. A quarter of Zinder's people starved, bands of children roamed the fields eating herbs and soil, tearing anthills apart for the stray seed or chaff they might find within. Dying parents left their children in the Zinder market in the hope that someone would take pity and feed them.

In fact, he said, gazing at us across the candles guttering in their clay sockets, he had heard stories of the market weeping with lost children, two hundred at a time.

Zinder, during the harmattan, was filled with the sound of coughing. Behind every wall people lay shivering with fever, unable to eat. By day, the wind never stopped, a high hot wind that blew the vultures backward through the sky and filled the air with a fine filter of dust. The lines of walls cast ambiguous shadows; the yellow neem leaves that lay scattered in the sand were blown to confusion by gusts that rose abruptly and set the door and shutters banging.

Every morning, three blind old women sang at the gate, faces raised to the sky, chanting the same words in one strong voice. Who would honor Allah, the source of all mercy and kindness, with a gift to his poor? Who would remember those who had risen to a day of hunger? Led by a little girl, they held tightly to the ends of three short sticks that linked them together in a chain. When Zara and Lizzy ran down to give them something, one woman raised a fist above her head to wish them a long life. Then they turned away, their shawls flapping behind them in the wind like great dark wings.

It was then, too, that waking slowly at night, we heard a solitary, plucked music that seemed to speak of the terrible unknowability of this place where Arab, European, and the old desert races had all mingled and strained to bring forth the blind child who extended a gaping bowl at noon, as oblivious of the past as of the future. Wounded city, wounded child, wearing its history like a bruise.

We had no idea of anything. But Delisse knew more. So we forgave him his exaggerated manner and the way he cut us short in the middle of a sentence. What could not be forgiven was the pain in his eyes that the lips pulled back over his bad teeth did nothing to dissemble.

The Hostel

The *gardien* who used to sit at the gate outside the hostel, the man who remembered Zara as a little girl, is not sitting in his usual place. On our way round to the door in back, past the bare concrete blocks and panes of glass streaked with dust, we hear the steady thud of wood on wood. Behind the hostel, on a sandy slope, a woman is pounding millet. A baby sags beneath the *pagne* wound around her back and looped at her breasts. The woman lifts the pestle above her head and lets it drop, bends and lifts again. She is standing in front of a hut, its rounded entrance, at this time of day, a solid black gash. The cone roof is spanned three times by narrowing circles of plaited straw: glossy gold, a swelling lifting to a point.

Beside the woman a little girl is holding a younger child on her hip, his legs straddling her waist. As we approach, he screams in terror, and the little girl jiggles him up and down, trying to make him hush. He hides his face in her neck, burrowing, but after a moment turns and peeks out.

The woman puts down the pestle and comes forward, calling to us. "*Sannu da zuwa,*" she says. We are greeted on our arrival. With one arm she reaches behind to hook the baby up a little and ties the cloth more securely above her breasts.

37

Zara knows her from the other visit here, and their questions and responses are prompted by warmth as well as courtesy. They are well and so am I, none of us is suffering from fatigue, the children are healthy, the heat is intense. We salute her on her work.

Greetings over, she tells us her news. The *gardien*, her husband, is dead of something in his stomach three months ago. He died in terrible pain. In a few weeks, she is going to return with the children to her family in Nguigmi.

This is shocking news to Zara, and she claps her hands together in surprise and sympathy.

Later on, underneath the revolving fan in the hostel, Zara will ask a question. By then, we will each have had a nap and will be struggling back into the longest moments of the unfinished day. The hostel will have taken on the familiar, doleful light of three o'clock in the afternoon.

But when we first come in out of the sun, it has the uncertain air of a place that someone has abandoned only a few moments before. In the front room, black flies are droning round the empty Pepsi bottles clustered on a low table under a slowly turning fan. In one corner there is a hot plate on a wooden table, and, on a shelf above, a cup with a spoon tipping out, an overturned pot, and a tin of Nescafé. In another corner, a bed stretches beneath a pair of windows. Each window, in its lead frame, is fastened shut with a hasp. The windows are too dusty to see through, useless.

Zara says she wants to sit for a while under the fan. There are three rooms in back, each opening onto the lofty porch that runs the length of the hostel. Each room has its Hausa bed and bare mattress, its white mosquito net tucked above. I stretch out on one of the beds, my head on the black leather bag, and fall instantly asleep.

My mother's bones are beginning their slow rise to the

surface of my dreams, bones clean as a whistle, dry as grass, are moving into the clean light of the sun, when I wake, my face stuck to the leather, and I can't remember where I am. It is too hot to move. Flies are droning around my ear, settling on my ankles and face.

And there, with the regularity of a heartbeat, is the hollow thud of wood on wood, the plunge into the vessel scooped from a single piece of dark wood. It reverberates in the pit of the stomach: the muffled boom, again, again. The relentless throb at the furthest point of the womb. The muscled clutch, the letting go. The deepest tick of all.

The baby is rocked to sleep, is rocked to waking, to hunger. Beneath the cloth the woman's breasts are filling with milk. The woman is alone now, making plans for her trip to Lake Chad. The sweat is standing on her forehead. Her arms lift and drop, this time, another: the tight kernel of grain is splintered, hewn. Her back, pulling against the heavy sink of the pestle, is embraced by tiny limbs, feet upturned at either side of her waist.

Later on she will sit feeding the baby on her lap, the baby will tug and grunt, she will stroke its head, pass her hand over its forehead. Wave away the flies. She will move the baby to the other side, encircle the baby with her arm.

This much is easy to know. For the rest, nothing. When she wakes in the morning, does she reach for the dead man before she remembers? Does she throw her arm out expecting it to land across his chest? Or is that gone now? Has his absence already become more familiar than all the years of sleeping side by side?

In the big room Zara is sitting with her feet on the table. Her eyes are closed. She has put her bag down on the floor and it is leaning against the leg of the chair. The Pepsi bottles have been cleared away and overhead the fan is slowly stirring the air. Behind Zara, a lizard scuttles along the wide reaches of the covered porch. He stops short, rigid, the tip of his orange tail curled against the painted brick red of the cement floor. Then up, down, up, down, his tiny front legs flex and pump. Again, still as death. Another moment and he has hurled himself forward, up through the wall of cement latticework and out onto the sand on the other side.

The great spaces of the porch are empty; in the dim corners of the ceiling, spiderwebs are floating free, long ragged threads come loose from their moorings.

There, where Zara's flip-flops are tilted against the edge of the table, the tape recorder once unleashed its sound. Where the flies still buzz round the sticky rings left by the bottles. She and Lizzy took turns pressing the start and stop buttons. Fingers that bent at the top joint, down. The backs of their knees pulled taut below the hems of their cotton dresses. Lizzy's hair was gathered in an elastic below each ear. When she lowered her head, the hollow at the base of her neck disappeared. Tulu sat on my lap, knees tucked snugly into my hands, knees roughened by their journeys over sand and cement.

The tape finished, we closed the door behind us and walked home. By then, the sky was a tender blue, the sand cooling beneath our feet. The enormous *gawo* tree opposite the Muslim cemetery was falling into shadow. In its thorny branches, vultures hunched against the fading light, waiting even then for the updrafts that would lift them into the sky again at dawn. Soon there would be the evening call to prayer and all over Zinder people would be thanking Allah for the gift of one more day, of one more moment in which to live and breathe.

"Quiet in here, isn't it," Zara says. Her voice is tentative, floating with the cobwebs.

"You're awake," I say, and sit down in the chair opposite, under the fan, and put my feet up on the table.

Zara's eyes are open, but they are focused inward, drugged with sleep. She looks at me, but not quite. "I was wondering," she says and stops. The blue scarf is lying in her lap and she has begun to pick absently at the knot. "I was wondering," she begins again, "if you remember my birthday."

I look at her, at a loss. Her birthday. Her eyes are on the knot, her fingers busy. Her hair is falling over her face. "I mean," she says, "do you remember my birthday that year we lived here in Zinder?"

I think for a minute. "I remember I was sick at the time," I say. "But I don't know if I remember the day itself. Somehow that whole time runs together. You were turning six and one of your front teeth had fallen out."

Zara nods, preoccupied, polite. Her question and my response are like the greetings, a preamble. She has undone the knot and is playing with the scarf now, winding it around her hand like a bandage. "But what is it?" I ask as quietly as I can. All at once I am full of dread.

Zara is silent. The fan is grinding overhead, ticking at the same point in each revolution. It wobbles on the ceiling, careening first toward one of us, then the other. "Oh, it's nothing," she says. "It's just that I was wondering if you remembered that day at all."

"We had a doll to give you on your birthday," I say. "A funny rubber one with arms and legs molded to her body. We found it before I got sick. I remember being glad of that, that we already had the doll. But Zara, tell me what you remember. Why do you ask?"

"It's a bit confused," she says, winding the scarf around her fist first one way, then the other. "I guess I don't remember the doll. But I remember Mme. Renault's, the children there all singing 'Joyeuse Anniversaire.' And Lizzy, she was with me." Zara pauses. "Then we came home," she says.

"And what happened?"

"Oh, nothing to speak of. Nothing that concerned anyone but myself. And you, a little. Not really an event at all. Nothing anyone else would have noticed."

"But then tell me," I insist.

She glances up, her dark eyes full of trouble. "Maybe another time," she says. "It's just that being here in Zinder brings things back. I didn't feel it so much a few months ago when I was here by myself, but today looking for the house together, it's different. My birthday—I can scarcely remember it myself. I don't really know. Maybe we can talk about it some other time."

A moment later, hands slack in her lap, she looks at me and smiles: a grimace, her mouth lifting at the corner. This is the same quick gesture of pain she made as a little girl, the notice that here is something I cannot fix. It is also the signal that for the moment there is nothing more to say.

But desperately wanting to fill the silence, not willing to bide my time, I am about to lead up to the subject in some other way, when I realize I am out of my depth. I have been with Zara in Matameye for three days. What do I know? Two years ago we stood in the airport and her ticket fluttered out of her hands and across the floor. I ran after it and handed it back, closed her fingers around the slippery paper. The questions stuck in my throat. Where are you going? And when, my daughter, will you return?

Nothing more to be said: how, then, to quell the rising panic, the unleashed imaginings? A child standing in the doorway, on the ledge. In her mouth a ragged space like the one in the smile of the little girl pulling herself through the sand. Out of sight, on the veranda, a brief still pool of shadows, fixing the hour. The sun goes down, the night comes up, a night so hot the sheets run quick as fire. There would have been sweat prickling the back of her neck, the delicate wings of her shoulders. Cased in by netting when escape must have seemed a willowed lake, the remembered taste of cherry popsicles on lips and tongue. Above, the four corners of the world caught motionless. An arm thrown blindly out, the desperate roll against the drooping net, and with the first light, a peppering of fragile death-carrying mosquitoes on the whitewashed wall beside the bed.

And here, in this room where we are now sitting, the wandering flute, the mournful oboe, the deep bravado of kettledrums: all supposed to have been a consolation for the sorrows of adult life, for the even more terrible griefs of childhood. To have been a place to go. The sheltering arms despaired of, the dear friend who appears just before it is too late. But most of all the morning meadow with its strains of rapture and delight, a reminder that in the end the wolf will be safely harnessed and the blithe going out into the meadow restored again and again.

This place is deserted, a forgotten heap of cinder block baking on its shelf of sand. It houses the fear that my child will someday find herself despairing and alone. All comfortless. That she'd prefer to die.

Before we leave the hostel, Zara and I make ourselves a cup of coffee. There is the little tin of Nescafé and a blue box of sugar cubes: St. Louis with the print of a red lion's head on the cover. We heat the water and pour it over the coffee grains. Then we each take a cube of sugar with us to dunk in the steaming coffee and go back and sit down under the fan.

"Do you remember," I ask Zara, "how we used to come up here to listen to *Peter and the Wolf?*"

"I think so," she says. The blue scarf is again tied firmly in place. "But I get that mixed up with someone who came to the gate once with a hyena on a chain. The hyena was wearing a muzzle but it was yanking at the chain and growling. Did that really happen?"

I think for a moment and tell her I remember that too: there was a man beating a drum and then the other one holding the chain.

"And children," Zara says. "There were a lot of children following them. Some were older than Lizzy and me. I can see them very clearly—running straight up to the hyena, then shrieking and running away."

"It must have been the harmattan," I say, "because there was so much sand in the air. A misty kind of day."

"I don't really remember," Zara says.

It is almost three-thirty now and we talk about setting off to find the house. There will be no difficulty; from the hostel I know exactly where it is. We wash our coffee cups and gather our leather bags. Will we ever again set foot together in this place? Surely not. I silently wish her a good life, as if we were parting for always. And the others. Goodbye, Lizzy, eyes growing dark at the sound of three horns, you sitting so quietly there with one thin leg crossed over the other. Goodbye, Tulu, with your rapturous thumping fists, your perfect timing. Goodbye, my darlings. Gone.

The House

At three-thirty in the afternoon, the sun is still very hot. It is moving west, the shadows on the sand are beginning to shift, but the air is still a harsh obstacle through which one moves with care. The straw hut in back of the hostel is dusty yellow. The mortar is standing outside, the pestle placed across its lip, yet the woman and her children are nowhere in sight. We pass through the gate and out onto the street, this time turning in the direction of the long stretch of sand that runs past our old house and continues all the way up to the Catholic mission.

But when we reach the junction I lose my bearings.

We might be looking across a watery waste, an expanse of solitude unbroken by a single vestige of the past. Instead of a *gawo* tree rooted in the sand, there is something that looks like a two-lane highway with a raised island running down the middle of it. On the island, at intervals, are long-necked sodium lights that lean out over the pavement. Between two of these lights, near where we are standing, is a kiosk with a sign over it that says *Glace*. Further down, at what must be the crossroads, we can see a large gas station. Green letters, BP, on a white field. At the moment there is not a single car or Land Rover or truck going anywhere, nor is there anyone at the kiosk. I know we are in Zinder because here is the sky, here is the sun. Goats are foraging in the sand at the edge of the cement. We are in the place we are looking for because the Catholic mission is still where it used to be, at the end of the road. But I am afraid to look more closely, to see if I can find the wall on the other side of the road, and then the gate in the wall, that opened to our house.

Like a child on the edge of sleep, whose first plunge into darkness jolts her awake, I clutch at the sheets of memory to salvage something from extinction. The skin around the children's eyes, smooth as glass. In the mirror the orange dust in the lines gathering around my own eyes.

"But this is the road we came in on," Zara tells me. "It leads straight up to the *auto gare*. Don't you remember?"

I remember nothing. Zara is sympathetic, obliging. "Never mind," she says. "We'll find the house. Don't worry."

There is no difficulty in crossing the wide expanse of empty concrete to the wall on the other side. We step up onto the island and then off again, squinting in the glittery light. Zara explains to me that she had never dreamed of looking here because one of the things she remembers is sitting with Lizzy on the wall outside our house and looking down into a long thoroughfare of sand that was certainly not a road.

Then she stops short, gazing down the length of concrete, clutching the strap of her leather bag that is hanging from her shoulder. She and Lizzy used to talk, she says, to a man who sat just below the wall cooking brochettes, *suya*, over a fire. But what they were doing, really, was waiting for the camels to pass. She tells me that this stretch of highway was built in honor of the Festival de la Jeunesse, which every other year is held in one of the departmental capitals. Last year it took place in Zinder, and she came up from Matameye to see it. Performers who had won competitions in their own villages and towns had assembled from all over Niger. There had been singers and wrestlers and groups of men and women dancers.

"Just there, down the road a little," she says, pointing, "is the Maison des Jeunes where most of the events were held. The highway," she says and laughs. "A little like building for the Olympics."

I had remembered a solid iron gate, but it doesn't matter. For our purposes, this one is better: solid only at the bottom, with bars crossing on top that allow us to look in. We can see a low whitewashed bungalow with a scrap of sand in front. The roof, a sheet of corrugated iron, overhangs four blunt pillars, but it is impossible to see beyond the pillars into the shadowy space behind. There is the cut of a door, dark against light: that is all. An open door. The brief interruption of a ledge. On the low platform of the house, between two pillars, a couple of clay flower pots are tipping in the sun. From where we stand, it is hard to tell if those are dried stems poking from them or mere twitchings of shadow. Yet we are close, only a few steps would take us across the patch of sand separating us from the house. A mortar bakes in the sun, the pestle leaning against it. Nearby, a little neem tree scatters a patch of mottled shade.

Zara and I are standing a little back from the gate, discreetly, in case anyone should appear at the door. We are standing full in the sun. My own back is running with sweat. I suppose hers must be as well. What she is thinking, I have no idea. Perhaps she will tell me her terrors, perhaps she will not. But of this, at least, I'm sure. I failed her, failed that one, the one with the empty place in her face, the one whose hand once rested in mine, the one who has disappeared from sight. The moments slipped through my fingers when I might have seen and did not.

And now, throbbing in the heat, running with the sweat down my back, a question: is it, once and for all, too late?

PART II   MATAMEYE

New Moon

Tambarin talaka cikinsa.
A poor man's drum is his belly.

What does one need to live?

A group of old women are sitting on a mat in the shade of a locust tree. They are talking about what is essential to life. One of them says this: "If you have no money, you can make do; without it you can survive. If you have no clothes, you can still manage; clothes are not necessary to life. But if your food is gone, then you will die."

Matameye is noisy with peacocks. A wealthy El Hadji who lives here brought them into the village. The spendthrift beauty of their tails seems a heady extravagance, a spectacular luxury, in a place where there is seldom enough millet to last from one harvest to the next. The peacocks scream at all hours of the day and night, flapping over the walls that separate one compound from another, picking everywhere for scraps. On the night of my arrival, after it has begun to cool, Zara and I go for a walk. We pass a *gawo* tree, its thorny branches full of roosting peacocks. Their tails are hanging

51

black against the fading yellow of the horizon. Overhead, where the sky has softened to a deeper blue, a new moon is brightening above the shadowy birds.

◈　　◈　　◈

A few days after our trip to Zinder, I visit Zara at the Centre Medical. She has told me to come late in the afternoon, sometime after four-thirty, when the heat is beginning to let up. This, I remember, is just past the hour of the third prayer, when an upright body casts a shadow the length of itself. I go out the corrugated iron gate in the banco wall and turn to the left, then turn left again and follow the road all the way to the end. Roads, in Matameye, are pathways bordered on either side by a continuous mud wall, sand lapping between: they are like corridors open to the sky. Overhead, vultures and black kites turn slowly against a naked blink of light. But the footprints inscribed in the sand below are beginning to fill with shadow: the pronged step of guinea fowl and the tiny cloven hoofmark of sheep and goats. A line of horseshoes. Or the shallow smudge of the naked human foot, the flat press of sandals.

Above the ruddy brown of the walls, neem trees lift their branches and drop yellow berries in the sand. The filmy leaves, sensitive to breezes, scatter watery patches of shade along the walls and on the mats placed beneath where old men sit cross-legged, fingering prayer beads. *"Ina wuni?"* they call out, greeting me on the afternoon. *"Ina gajiya?"* They smile and nod, rewind their turbans. A boy is bringing his neighbor's goats back from the fields. They trot bleating through the sand, one by one disappearing into doorways, like good children returning home from school. The last safely behind a wall, the boy joins a group of other boys playing soccer. One of them wears a flat stick tied firmly to the stump of his thigh, and when the ball bounces in front of him, he whacks it with his wooden leg, sending it high above the heads of the others. Then he rests a hand on his hip, casual.

Behind the walls stretch compound after compound, each with its doorway, its courtyard, its inner rooms or huts. Each entrance opens to a vestibule, an anteroom called a *zaure,* and it is here that visitors leave behind their sandals. From the path where I am walking, it is easy to catch a glimpse into the courtyards beyond. A woman is standing over a mortar, her back straightening and bending with the lift and plunge of the pestle. A baby is tied to her back, and it looks out with sleepy eyes above the cloth looped at her breasts. Dreaming, rocked, its feet upended on either side of her waist, it makes a pillow of her spine. Against the far wall, behind a fire nestling a black pot, several calabashes tip forward in the sun. One is half full of golden meal, fresh from the mortar, to be added later to the pot of *tuwo.* Another holds the raw grain, the unbroken millet seed.

Where a narrow path crosses the wider one that sweeps up to the Centre Medical, a little domed mosque sits on a corner. In its small patch of praying ground a *malam,* surrounded by children, sits with an inkpot between his knees. He is showing a child who stands beside him how to make Arabic letters on a wooden scroll. The other children are sitting barefoot at his feet, scrolls in their laps, flip-flops left behind, two by two, at the edge of the mat.

On the opposite corner is the hut Zara and I passed last night on our walk. In front an old woman had sat on a mat selling groundnuts; they were arranged in groups of six or seven, each pile neatly contained in a little round tin. Zara told me her name is Deje, and that she lives alone, making her living by selling the groundnuts to people who sometimes pass. Against the protests of her children and grandchildren who remain in Kano where they were born and where her husband died, she has returned to Matameye because it is here she was a child. We had stopped to greet her, and she had lifted open hands to each side of her face, tapping the air over and over in welcome. Her breasts hung in neat flaps above the cloth that covered her from waist to feet. She had taken Zara's hand and had peered, beaming, first into my face, then into hers. *"Uwarki,"* she had said: your mother. When Zara had opened her change purse and brought out the coin to buy some groundnuts, Deje had smoothed a piece of brown paper and spilled into it one little nest of groundnuts after another, emptying all her stock. Then she had pressed the coin back into Zara's hand; we must take these as a gift of welcome on the occasion of my arrival.

As I pass now, Deje is nowhere in sight. The hut is quiet, but from behind it there is a rustle and a peacock steps daintily backward, tail spread in quivering splendor, blues and greens flashing darkly like jewels under water.

The Centre Medical is a long, low building set a little back from the tarred road that runs down from Takieta on its way to Kano. Locust trees throw dappled shadows on the sand and on the yellow walls, on the slatted shutters propped open to let in the light. A veranda runs along the front arranged with benches where two boys are sitting, looking out at the road.

I sit down to rest, and after a moment a dwarf crosses from the other side to join a group of men talking under a tree. He comes slowly forward, rolling from side to side. When he is standing with the others in the shade, one of the group, a man they are calling Aboubakar, reaches down and takes his hand. Aboubakar begins to tell the dwarf a story, and as he talks he swings their coupled hands back and forth between them. The dwarf listens, head at a tilt. When he laughs, his forehead wrinkles in long lines of sympathy.

After a few minutes a man steps from inside the Centre onto the veranda where we are sitting, his head ducking beneath the frame of the door. He must be seven feet tall. Aboubakar looks up, drops the dwarf's hand, and gives a shout. He waves the giant over to where they are standing and lines the dwarf up against him. The dwarf comes to just above the giant's knees. The giant lowers his hand and rests it lightly on the dwarf's shoulder. Around them, everyone laughs and exclaims while the dwarf holds perfectly still, smiling. After a few minutes the giant ambles off down the street and the dwarf stays talking with the others, his head dropped far back on his neck, his little arms crossed in front of him.

Inside the entrance is a little office, dark even during mid-afternoon, belonging to the Majeur, the nurse who oversees all the work of the Centre. And beyond his office, a long room with a table down the middle, a standing scale in one corner, and a poster on the wall showing a woman with a sick child in her lap. *"Donnez à boire,"* it says, *"pour que le diarrhée ne fatigue pas votre enfant."* Beside it, another poster is tacked up, this time of two women, each holding a child. One child is emaci-ated. *"Mangeant que le mils"* are the words above. The other child is the picture of health. The caption reads: *"Mangeant une varieté."*

In this room, under a revolving fan, Zara and her coworker, Hadiza, are weighing pregnant women and taking their blood pressure. Hadiza is tall and very thin. Markings so fine they might have been etched with the fine point of a pen reach from the corners of her mouth all the way up to her temples. When she smiles, they disappear in the lines of her face. This is the afternoon for prenatal care; tomorrow babies will be weighed in the cradle scale now standing idle on the table. I sit down, and when the next woman enters, Zara hands me her *carnet*. The woman's body is given delicate attention: the weights on the scale are positioned exactly and a band tied around her arm. A moment later Zara calls out a number and I write it down. Just outside the door, a step away, women are waiting on benches under the neem trees. They sit talking quietly, swatting the flies away—with a flap of their *pagnes*—from the babies dozing on their laps.

At the end of the afternoon, when we are about to leave, a woman arrives who is not pregnant. She has not come to be weighed, but for help of another kind. She unloops the front of her *pagne* and unwinds from inside an infant, a girl child, who is all bones. Her head is a tiny skull, the four plates distinct, the deep crevice of the fontanel pulsing between. Her legs are jointed sticks, the kneecaps spools of bone. Around one ankle is a bracelet woven from pink yarn, and around her neck, wrinkled as an old woman's, is a string from which hang little leather amulets placed there for her protection. She breathes slowly and with an effort. When Hadiza feels her tiny arms for the soft droop of dehydration, the baby begins crying, a thin piteous cry, broken and breathless, her dark eyes fastened on her mother's face. The mother rocks her slowly in her hands. Has the mother any milk of her own? Hadiza asks. Hadiza's voice, when she speaks, lapses into sighs and small gasps of surprise. Now it cracks on the word *nono:* milk. None, the woman shakes her head. Then, Hadiza says, she must give the baby some goat's milk; she must get some and give it to the baby right away. And she herself, that her milk may return, must eat beans as well as millet; she must try to remember that this is important for the baby as well as for herself. The woman nods, her eyes on her child, and Hadiza, catching her breath, begins explaining all over again what she must do. The woman continues to nod, goat's milk, yes, beans, legumes. When Hadiza has finished speaking, she bends over and centers the baby on her back, covers it with her *pagne*, and leaves.

There is another woman waiting who has kept quietly outside the door. She comes in now, carrying in her arms a child whose legs are hugging her waist. He is naked and it is impossible to guess his age. His mother leans down and places him carefully on the scale, steadying him. His ribs stand out like the rake of a plow, his lips are pulled back in a death grin. He sways when she moves her hands, his knees wide open. From beneath drooping eyelids, he looks slowly from one of us to another. His gaze is deliberate, touching each in turn. Zara, this time, jiggles the weights of the scale while his mother looks up from where she squats beside him. There is no mention of kilos and grams, but Zara explains what can be done for dehydration. His mother must make a solution of water with a pinch of salt and four cubes of sugar and must feed it to him with a dipper, drop by drop. She must do this all day long, "*ɗuk rana sosai*," from dawn to dusk. And at night, too, she must do the same, must drop water on his tongue hour by hour without ever forgetting. This is necessary if he is to grow strong, Zara says, "*kamar haka*," like this, and she clenches her fists in front of her and tightens the muscles of her arms in a show of strength.

This woman, too, nods and listens, but never takes her eyes from the child. She listens to Zara with a kind of embarrassed attention, as if prevented by politeness from saying what she knows. The child has been sitting perfectly still, his breath coming in shallow gasps. Now he makes an effort to move the hand that is resting on his knee. Slowly, he reaches between his legs until his hand comes to rest on the tender droop of his genitals. It stays there, holding on. Is the child's father nearby? Zara asks. The woman turns to look at her and shakes her head, no; he went away during the drought to find work and hasn't returned. Do you have any money? Zara asks. The woman looks away again, ashamed. Zara takes a few coins from her change purse and gives them to her. The woman receives them with cupped hands, then carefully knots them into a corner of her *pagne*. It is time now to leave, and she picks up the child, settling him on her hip. But at the door she turns and looks from me to Zara, then back again to me. Holding my eyes with her own, her child staring from her hip, she raises a tight fist above her head, thumb up, and slowly shakes it in greeting.

When they are gone, Zara tells me that only last week she had played with this child, had poked her head out from beneath the blue scarf and made him smile. He is two and a half years old. Impossible, I say, and she asks how old I had thought he was. His eyes had the look of someone to whom the worst had been done, who was no longer capable of surprise. But I scarcely gave his age a thought. There had been the moment of shocked disbelief, the horrified blink, then the tearing at the bottom of the self, the terrible surge from beneath of sobs, immediately checked and forbidden. Goat's milk for the baby, but why did Hadiza say it over and over? Couldn't she see there wasn't a minute to lose? And Zara: what could she be thinking of? The child swaying on the scale was half-dead; how could she go on and on as if there were all the time in the world? But even then, outraged and incredulous, I knew that my own most frantic wish, the appalled need of my reason, was that these children be removed from my sight at once, that their mothers without a moment's delay wrap them in their *pagnes* and take them to a place from which they could never return.

But the gesture that stopped the heart was his hand, as he sat there on the scale, scarcely able to move, scarcely able to lift his eyes, his hand reaching out to touch his withered scrotum. I won't, the swooning reason had pleaded, won't follow this further. He cannot hurt, cannot feel, already he is beyond it all, his suffering must be over. But no. In that gesture, so human, so male, he was proved, beyond every impassioned argument to the contrary, a human creature in need of comfort, one of our own. A loose collection of bones pitifully clothed in skin, a boy.

There are not enough questions, not enough words in which to ask them. How? I ask Zara. Tell me what you know. She says that the longer she is here, the more it eludes her. There is a drought and afterward there is a famine. There is not enough to eat. That much is clear. It is now the beginning of August, the granaries are empty, the harvest, rich or poor, will not be gathered for a couple of months. But that is not all. Children develop diarrhea and fevers, and, in a climate such as this, quickly become dehydrated. The parents, overworked, uncertain what to do, and too far away to make the trip easily, do not bring them to the clinic right away and they begin to lose weight. The slide into malnutrition is rapid. Soon too weak to eat, they turn away from food altogether. They must be coaxed to take a bite of food, must be fed water spoonful by spoonful. Their mother's milk dries up, there's no longer even that. So if they weren't dehydrated to begin with, they become so. A vicious cycle.

And then, she says, quite apart from diarrhea and lack of food, although not unrelated, are weaning customs. At the age of nineteen months many children are given for a time to their grandmothers, are removed suddenly from their mothers and their milk. Pining, despondent, they may lose their appetite. Zara says she has seen many children come to the clinic whose malnourishment seems to have set in during the last half of their second year. But at the root of it, she says, whatever the immediate cause, famine or custom or disease, is poverty. Not having enough of what's needed. These women who come in from villages in the bush may walk miles every day to a well and carry the water home on their heads, as well as work in the fields beside their husbands when the rains begin. They suffer from exhaustion, cannot always care for the child they know is in distress. They may even, sometimes, turn away from the child.

"I don't begin to understand it all," she says. "But the root is poverty."

Then she tells me about the first death from starvation she witnessed, a three-year-old child named Maria who was staying in the little house they call the hospital in back of the Centre. Every day Maria's mother held her in her arms, rocking her, calling her by name. The father stood by, at a loss, asking what the child needed, what he could do. But she was beyond it all, her mouth by then was bleeding and she could barely whimper. One morning Zara came to work and was told the child had died during the night. The mother was sitting looking out at the field behind the hospital and when Zara approached her she began to weep silently, the tears running down her face. The father was outside, shoveling a grave.

But how do people go on waking to the call to prayer, spooning out the *tuwo*, calling their greetings back and forth all day long; how does Matameye get from one day to another, with the children dying behind its walls, beneath its *pagnes*? That is what I want to ask Zara. Why doesn't it raise its fist against the sky, collapse in despair, lie down in the sand and never get up? Shriek to the rest of the world that there are bones here burning like embers. Demand the superflux be shaken to show the heavens more just.

Although I use no words, Zara responds as if I had. "But you know," she begins, then stops, looking straight at me for a moment, eyes abashed. "You know," she begins again, "Matameye is a bountiful place. There's an overflow of something here, whatever it is that keeps us all afloat. I suppose you could call it a lot of things: energy, humor, generosity. But the word I use to myself"—and here again she pauses, as if taking a breath before revealing the secrets of her soul—"is joy."

Beneath it all, the astonished gasp: who is this Zara, a Zara I have never seen before? Not a girl at all, a woman with her head bent over a baby. A woman I can scarcely recognize. Altogether different, again, from the Zara who walked beside me a few days ago in Zinder, our feet keeping time, a Zara who even then knew more than she could say. And where, suddenly, did it come from, her bright way with children, her instinct to play? Clapping her hands softly in front of her? Peeking out from behind the blue scarf? How, in the face of such desperation, can she think of such things?

Piteous beyond words, the gulf between the image of a robust, energetic child summoned by Zara's tightened fist, her words, "*kamar haka*," and the swaying child on the scale. But she is matter-of-fact, getting on with it.

And matter-of-factly, as we part to go to bed, Zara tells me she is glad I have come to Matameye.

That night, in Zara's little house, I wake to a dream of a woman standing with her back to me, a child straddling her hips. But when she turns to face me, I see it is my mother. Too hot to breathe, too hot to open my eyes, I burrow beneath the smell of sweat and dust for that other smell buried in the yellow sheets, the fragrance of lost gardens. The air is brimming gold in the long light of a summer afternoon. She is holding me, my mother, holding me up to the mortal beauty of the hour. Her arms are around me, her hair is silky on my cheek. Beneath her feet the earth is pure loam.

I want my mother, the one who held me in her arms. There's the snapshot to prove it, my mother in a white dress, shadows running across it in dark stripes, holding me, her baby, in a garden. All around us, trees are spilling light. Roses bow beneath the weight of bees and small white butterflies are dancing above lavender and loosestrife. Her dark hair is glinting, her face is mild. She is looking straight into the eye of the camera, trying not to squint. Me, the baby on her arm, is crowing with delight, all sunshine.

Swaddled in a linen sheet, my winding cloth, my shroud. Coiled in a burning nest, knees drawn to chin. Sing a song of robins, of cherries in the rain. Stricken hearts of peonies, five o'clocks in flames. Forget me not, my mother, milkweed in a pod. Hollyhock along the hedge, sweet peas in the shade. Rockabye this baby, sing her a song. Still through the hawthorn blows the cold wind.

Moon in First Quarter

Ba ɗon tuwo aka yi ciki ba.
It is not for food that the insides were created.

Every night before we go to sleep, Zara and I sit looking up into the sky. The chairs rest on a cement platform that juts out from the house, a ramp floating lightly above the sand. We sit deep in the plastic string hatches of the chairs, knees drawn up, feet resting on the top rungs. We talk of this and that, but often say nothing at all. Most nights the sky leans so close that conversation seems an interruption. The Milky Way flows just above our heads, a discrete river of light in a sky of clear deep blue.

One evening, soon after I arrive, El Gouni, the woman who lives on the other side of the wall, comes to visit. At the gate she claps twice, sharply, then comes forward out of the shadows. The moon is setting beyond the wall, disappearing like the sudden quick slide of the evening sun. "El Gouni," Zara says, rising quickly and going to meet her. She is a large woman, older than myself, with wide gums and straight white teeth. She is carrying a bottle of oil, corked with a twist of brown paper, a gift of welcome. Her neck is creased, her fingers delicate on the neck of the bottle. Again and again she greets me: *Sannu ɗa zuwa, sannu, sannu, sannu.* She says how glad everyone is that Zara's mother has come, how they have waited for my visit. She hopes that I am not too tired from my journey and that I am now finding rest. Keeping one hand on Zara's wrist, she looks eagerly back and forth from one of us to the other.

Sit down, Zara tells her, pushing forward the string-backed chair. But El Gouni shakes her head, and lowers herself instead onto the Hausa bed placed under the branches of the neem tree in case someone should wish to sleep outside. If the chair is good, she says, this is better, and rocks over to stretch her length for a moment on the hard, slatted bed.

I have been trying to remember what Zara has told me about El Gouni and now I do. During Zara's first days in Matameye, the old women sitting along the path to the Centre Medical called out to her as she passed, putting their hands to their breasts and asking where was her mother. When she answered that her mother was far away, they shook their heads and said if she had any trouble she must be sure to come to them; they would take care of her. But it is to El Gouni, she said, she would turn. She wakes up to the sound of her pounding, and in the middle of the day falls asleep to it. If she were sick or frightened, all she would have to do is call out, and El Gouni would hear. And she confides in El Gouni. Almost every evening on her way back from the Centre, Zara says, she stops to see her, to talk about things that have happened during the day and to hear what she has to say. I had felt, hearing this, a rush of jealousy. Was another woman beginning to take my place? Perhaps Zara would make comparisons, prefer a woman who was wiser than myself. Who could comfort her, advise her, in ways I didn't know how.

After a few minutes, El Gouni straightens, placing her hands together in her lap, palms up, one inside the other. She begins by talking about the rains, how there have been better years, but also worse. There was a good rain yesterday, El Gouni says, nodding from one of us to the other. She only hopes it didn't come too late.

Zara turns to look at me and my heart sinks. The words, "too late," let loose on the air the anxiety that has become my habitual companion, unlatch my fear that I can never make up to Zara for the failures of the past, that whatever happened on her sixth birthday can have no sequel.

But no, for the time being Zara is turning to me only in recognition—the rain, she murmurs—of the moment yesterday when we had been returning from the market just as a fierce wind sprang up. We covered our faces as best we could and walked bowed against the needling sand. From far away, we heard a low rumble, then, almost immediately, a sudden, deafening clap of thunder just above our heads. We were barely through the gate, inside the house, when the skies opened and the rain fell. Immediately we had pulled two chairs up to the door, as if a play were beginning, and sat looking out. Water dropped in a sheet, a blind silver screen.

El Gouni tells me what Zara related the first night I arrived, that only a month ago Matameye was still waiting for the rains to begin. Her Hausa is very clear, very deliberate, so I can understand without too much difficulty, filling in with what I already know, when she explains that the first crop of millet had been planted, a false rain or two had fallen, then there was nothing. There would be the usual violent gusts of wind springing from nowhere, the fierce scattering of sand, but then, while everyone listened to the thunder roll across the sky, the winds would drop. Meanwhile, the precious grain rotted in the fields. Every night all of Matameye would assemble for prayers, beseeching Allah not to forget them. No one, passing in the streets, talked of anything else. By the time the rains finally did begin, the first planting had been lost.

Zara is looking back and forth between El Gouni and me, one on either side of her. The bottle of oil corked with brown paper is resting beside the leg of her chair, and as she gazes at one of us, then the other, she turns the bottle between her fingers. Suddenly El Gouni smiles at me widely, the gums showing above her perfect teeth. It is very good I have come, she says. All of Matameye has been waiting to see Zara's mother. Sometimes Zara seems her own beloved child—in fact, she says, sometimes she forgets Zara has another mother—and she will weep, as will all of Matameye, on the day Zara leaves.

I am gathering myself, trying to decide whether what she has said makes things better or worse, when she turns to Zara and, speaking so rapidly that I know she has been carefully enunciating for my benefit, relates something that makes Zara clap her hands together once in excitement. "*Kai!*" she exclaims.

"It's Marianma," Zara says, turning to me, attuned to what I can understand and what I cannot. "She's coming soon to stay with El Gouni for a week or two. I'm sure you'll still be here. You'll see her." Then, turning back to El Gouni, she says she knows El Gouni must already be counting the days.

I wonder how I can have forgotten. When Zara told me that El Gouni had become a kind of mother to her, she had also told me about Marianma, El Gouni's own daughter. She looks like a very young girl, she had said, but in fact is a woman in her mid-twenties. Seven pregnancies, seven babies, all dead. The first lived a year and a half, another six months. Others died at birth. A strange and terrible fate, Zara had said, frowning a little, even here, where babies die so easily. To have looked on each of their faces and then have them snatched away. Can you imagine the yearning in her heart, she had asked me, the sense of having been betrayed? I saw her after the death of the last, she continued. What was pitiful was that when people greeted her, she made an effort to respond. It was as if she were being dragged out of a dream, as if she were trying to wake up but couldn't. That's what I saw, Zara had said, as if stating it for herself.

Then she told me that Marianma's husband is a good man, you could see he loved her. He could hold her gaze when she turned away from every other. But then she began undergoing periods when she recognized no one, when she seemed to be holding a conversation deep within herself. Now Marianma often stays in the village where she lives with her husband, about two days' journey from Matameye, sequestering herself, sometimes eating nothing, drinking nothing. And she is a clever seamstress, embroiders beautifully; she can keep an entire pattern in her head, whole complicated designs. But she no longer comes regularly, as she once did, to visit El Gouni.

"I pity her very much," Zara had said, shaking her head.

El Gouni beams at me again, her elbows planted on her knees, taking my goodwill for granted. "Marianma is my daughter," she says simply. Then, abruptly changing the subject, she asks me how Zara's father is, my husband. She listens carefully to my answer that he was well when I left him, that he was sorry not to be able to come with me to visit Matameye, then tells us that a cowife who has been married to her husband three times, always leaving, is returning within the week. She and this woman never got on together but they are both older now, and she hopes will have learned something.

We all lapse into silence, listening to the slow pulse of the cicadas. While we have been talking in the dark, the early moon has disappeared over the wall. Now the stars fill the sky entirely.

"But what do they matter, these differences," El Gouni says, meditatively. "We're all the same, anyway. We all have eyes," she says and points to her own. "We all have a nose," touching hers, and then, pointing down, "we all have a vagina."

Zara laughs, surprised, and looks to see if I have understood. El Gouni laughs too, protesting. "Well, we're all women here, aren't we?" Then she says, "And what we all want is the same, too: the peace that Allah gives. But for that we must pray without ceasing."

We are silent again, each thinking her thoughts. The sky is a depthless blue, reaching further and further away from this small space where we are sitting. Then lightly, glancing at El Gouni, Zara says she knows how to pray. She bows her head, hair falling in a screen, and places her palms together. But El Gouni laughs and says no, she doesn't know how to pray. She doesn't even know that she must pray with her face turned east, in the direction of Mecca.

"Then you must teach me," Zara says.

When El Gouni has put her third cloth over her head and departed, Zara tells me that although El Gouni has never learned to read or write, now she is learning Arabic so that she will be able to read the Qur'an for herself. She is devoted to her prayers, although, apparently, this has not always been the case. She has told Zara that when she was a young woman she took no interest. "And you," Zara asks, turning to me in the dark, "growing up the way you did. Do you think about these things, too?"

Well might Zara ask. Certainly while she was a child at home, I turned my back on it all, the Catholicism that had run like a river beneath my own young days, the injunction to pray without ceasing.

But how is this to be done?

The pilgrim's question, asked of stranger and friend, in village and town, from one end of the forest to the other. He had read that we must always and everywhere pray with uplifted hands. At dawn; again in the middle of the day when accidie, the demon of noontide, is abroad; and throughout the hours of darkness. "I sleep, but my heart wakes." Pray with every breath, every beat of the pulse, in company and in solitude, in the pride of youth and the debility of age, in the complacencies of harvest and in the harrowing moment of need.

Every morning before it is light, Matameye is awakened by the call to prayer. "*Allahu akbar, Allahu akbar. Ashhadu an la ilaha illal lah. Ashhadu an la ilaha illal lah.*" The *mu'azzin*'s voice quavers high on the long vowels, comes up short against the rolled *r*'s. Five times a day, the reminder that Allah is supreme and that the moment has come to pray with one's heart and one's lips. The call to *salla* is always the same, except that before daybreak, when the call shatters the solitary dreaming world of bodies stretched on mat or bed, a phrase is added: "*As-salatu khayra min an nawm.*" Prayer is better than sleep.

While Matameye is rising to the ablutions that cleanse it for prayer, washing hands and feet, mouth, nostrils and ears, I lie still between my mother's yellow sheets and wonder what I am doing here and what has brought me to this place, of all others, where men and women and children wake each morning to famine and to belief, as did my Irish ancestors, shivering in a bog.

Kurum ita ma magana ce.
Silence, too, is talk.

The morning Zara and I traveled up from Matameye to
Zinder, something happened that I prefer to forget. In the flat
land surrounding the city where the outcroppings of rock rise
buoyant on either side of the road, our *taxi brousse* was stopped
by a gendarme. He was dressed in khaki, a red felt beret tipped
forward on his forehead. Behind him, under the branches of
an acacia tree, another gendarme was stretched in the heat on
the springs of an iron-frame bed stuck in the sand. The driver
was asked to produce his papers. While he was looking for
them in a dusty brown envelope, the gendarme put his head in
the window. He observed the women with children sleeping
on their laps, the old men in turbans, the lidded enamel pots—
the *kwanos*—tied with pieces of cloth. Then he looked at Zara
and me, our identical black leather bags flat on our knees, and
fired a question at me. I didn't understand what he was saying. Zara answered for me, in Hausa, no, we didn't have anything to declare, nothing. Then he looked back and forth
between Zara and me and rapidly said something to which
she had replied with a shrug.

"What did he say?" I asked her.

"Well," she began, and stopped.

"It was something about me, wasn't it?"

"Oh, just something about speaking Hausa. How I'm more fluent, that's all."

"And how odd that is, given the fact I'm older." I saw in her face I had guessed correctly. "It's true," I said lightly. "It's perfectly true."

Oh no, neither one of us need take this too seriously. That's what her shrug and my dismissive acknowledgment are meant to say. But I can imagine her confusion, and my own face burns with shame. Perhaps we are both relieved the truth has been stated at last. El Gouni, for example, was much too discreet to make comparisons. She nodded encouragingly the other night when I tried to speak. Privately, Zara and I say to each other that I am seventeen years away from the language, that she lives in a setting where she can go for days without speaking either English or French. We say that Zinder is another case altogether. But how far can remarks of this kind take us? In themselves, they point to the need for an explanation. Eagerly, I study the book in the mornings, make an effort to speak when we go out. Listen closely to night visitors. For her part, Zara explains idioms. She tells me how much I understand, how I'm learning day by day.

But the soldier's remark sends the blood flying to my face. After all, what was I doing the year we lived in Zinder? That is the question that looms between Zara and me. For what, all that drugged scrutiny of dark on light, that rapt surrender to the seduction of shadows? Of what was I thinking? It is not enough to say that instead of working in a clinic I was spending my days with Lizzy and Tulu and herself. That doesn't answer it. All of Zinder waited beyond the gate. Zinder, voiced, exuberantly verbal. In the face of it, I made of the little girls my safety. When we went out, I clung to their small hands as fervently as they clung to mine. At home, it was Mike who sat talking to visitors, asking questions and answering them, laughing and exclaiming.

"But you were doing other things," Zara had said the night we returned from Zinder and were sitting again in the string-backed chairs beneath the stars. "Think of all the time you spent with us."

Zara opens the conversation without any allusion to the soldier's remark; she knows it is unnecessary. She wants to reassure me that my life has not been lived in vain. That the days spent slogging through the sand have added up to something: herself. And of course I have only to look at her sitting there with her legs stretched out in front of her, her face turned to mine, to know I could want nothing more.

This may be the sum of it. But as so often happens, Zara's uneasiness seems to match my own. "There's not an instant of that time I regret," I say.

I speak spontaneously, vehemently, and know I am telling the truth. It's certainly not the time spent with the little girls I regret. It's the cost to Zara and to the others of what might be called—in kindness if not in truth—my inattention; and the cost to myself of a deep-seated timidity before the world. What was it, in Zinder, all those years ago, that kept me from speaking? It may have been a simple case of lethargy. Or fear. Was I afraid I couldn't learn the words? That I would be shamed? On the other hand, perhaps it was the eager faces I was afraid of, the naked look of comprehension. The accurate gesture of hand or eye that would have left me blazing in the sun. Or a dream, forgotten before it was remembered, that seventeen years later a gendarme would stick his head into a *taxi brousse* and declare my ignorance.

"And as for Niger," Zara continues, "what I notice is how at ease you are here. How much at home you seem."

Zara has a good heart. She takes no pleasure in perceiving my confusion. The keen pleasure of having routed a parent on her own ground is short-lived, I know. Soon enough fear creeps in. Does she pity me for what may seem to her my lost opportunities? Is her own ardent grasp of the present a determined effort to spare herself regrets?

Yet even her attempt to reassure me of the continuity, the fullness, of my experience, only sets throbbing the wound that the past few days have inflicted: the fretful knowledge that I have lost Zara to a world in which I am entirely a stranger. That despite my brief passage here, years ago, it is a world I see now to be altogether unknown to me, a world of which I learned nothing. That where Zara has useful work here in Matameye, has discovered another language, even another mother of sorts, I, in the face of harrowing famine, spend my days idly, have only a few words of entry, and have found no other child, here or elsewhere. Even Zinder, the beloved city where I was sure I could find my way, the city where it had seemed inevitable that Zara and I should meet, has, despite our best intentions, proved an estrangement. The child, Zara, has been irretrievably lost, and Zara of the present has disappeared into a world in which I recognize nothing.

Tsoro na ɗaji kunya ta giɗa.
Fear in the forest is shame in the house.

First thing in the morning, Zara is up taking a shower. I lie in bed, pretending to be still asleep. I know that after her shower she likes to sit in front of the house and drink a solitary cup of coffee. She has described that in a letter, how she likes sitting in one chair with her feet up on another listening to the sounds of early morning: the sturdy thud of El Gouni's pestle, the coos and sighs of doves hidden in the neem leaves, and from nearby, the voices of women, calling to each other over the walls. At a distance of six thousand miles it had seemed easy enough to imagine. Now I can see there had been something ideal about the picture, something spare and unfurnished. What had I known of all the rest, everything that came before? The slap of flip-flops on the cement floor, the metallic clank of the handle hitting the bucket she fills so there will be water at noon when the town supply is cut off, the large plastic aquamarine mug, ridged down the sides to prevent its slipping from the fingers. Or, for that matter, the undisturbed glass plate on the shelf beside the mug, a plate exactly like the one she ate from as a child in Zinder.

Nor had I foreseen my own stealthy presence in the bed, covered modestly with a sheet to protect my child from a chance and startling glimpse of the body that was her first home. For a time she was my guest and now I am hers. I have had no practice in this, visiting a grown child, and it is sometimes hard to remember who she is and who I am, to miss this most obvious point, that we are mother and daughter. When we walk through the streets, people look up and smile: here at last is Zara with her mother, walking beside the womb from which she struggled to take the first free breath of her life. But sometimes I feel my own face go stiff with embarrassment and I must suppose that Zara feels the same. Perhaps her fear is that however far she may go, and for however long, this loose arrangement of flesh and bone will be stalking her like a shadow, reminding her of where she came from. That she will never be permitted to forget the raging hunger that woke her in the night and which for a brief period I alone could satisfy.

And my own fear? That I shall never recover from her brief tenancy of a body now in decline, that housing her limbs, meeting her thirst, has left me a creature distraught. How am I to forget the frantic cries that night after night jolted me from dreams that gradually took on the dark tones of disaster? The helpless body, limp as life, whose rescue from starvation depended on my renouncing the self sought in sleep and turning to her with full breasts? How is it possible for either of us to recover from an intimacy such as ours?

Zara's closest friend in Matameye is a woman named Maimoun, pronounced "my moon." In letters Zara described the immediate chord of sympathy struck between them when they first met at the Centre, where, for a time, Maimoun came every day to visit her sick mother. In the morning Maimoun would arrive with dishes containing *tuwo* and sauce made from tomatoes and onions and baobab leaves, whatever she knew her mother liked best. Then she would sit with her, making sure she ate it. Zara, coming and going in the room also occupied by malnourished children, saw Maimoun often, and right away was drawn by something watchful and amused in her expression. When the mother left the Centre, they arranged to visit each other, and as Zara learned to speak Hausa more fluently their conversation became increasingly intimate. In fact, it was to exchange stories about things that had happened to them as children, to gossip about people they both knew, or to recount dreams and stray impressions, that Zara had tried so hard to learn the language. And Maimoun, on her side, had been Zara's best teacher, the one who had intuitively understood what she wanted to say and helped her to say it. When they were together in a group of people, talking, Maimoun had sat beside her, isolating the word or expression she was aware Zara wouldn't understand and explaining it to her. They are known to be close friends in Matameye, and people often ask one of them for news of the other. Maimoun and Zara are the same age, twenty-three, but Maimoun has been married since she was thirteen and now has five children.

One night, sitting under the stars, Zara tells me about the children I will soon meet. There is the baby, Fasuma, and then three older ones, two boys and a girl. The eldest is a daughter, ten years old, who does not live with Maimoun and her husband, Sani. She lives instead with Maimoun's mother, an arrangement not at all uncommon with a first child. Talatuwa visits often, sometimes every day, but she is treated very differently from the others. Maimoun, a rapt and thoughtful mother, with Talatuwa is brusque. Talatuwa carries water and bathes the younger children. But instead of thanking her, Maimoun is critical. Why does she walk in such a clumsy manner? Doesn't she know how to stand up straight? But Maimoun, Zara protests, think how she must feel.

"I've learned that with many firstborn children it's the same," Zara tells me, tipping her head back to look straight up into the sky. "Some constraint there, what people call shame. The word they use is *koumia.* Parents won't speak the name of an eldest child, not directly to the child or to anyone else. We can be weighing babies and will ask for a baby's name. The mother will bow her head in silence and everyone calls out, '*Koumia ta ke ji.*' Then another woman will pronounce the name."

Of course Zara does not say what we are both thinking, that here we are, a mother and a firstborn child. Although I ask questions as if all this is surprising to me, even shocking, I am neither surprised nor shocked. Rather, I am embarrassed, and in this turning away, this blush immediately disguised as innocence, I am reminded of my own confusion down on the coast in Lagos before Zara was born and for a time afterward. Shame is the right word, exactly, and I wonder now that I have not stumbled on this knowledge before.

Only once, but that is enough, the final shattering of virginity, the unknowing body taken by surprise. Only once, the startled gesture of recoil, the abashed turning aside from so thorough and irrevocable a violation of the space around one's skin.

There was that: nights lying awake, her body shifting beneath the skin of mine. Shutters flung wide, the moon in the window, the leaves of the frangipani tree in a season of harmattan coated with dust. A silver streak of light passing over the glossy planks of the mahogany floor and up the wall. Pausing on the dark wardrobe standing in the corner, on the body naked beside me in the bed. Then, a single gleam in the deep embrasure of the window and the room again fell into shadow. Outside, everything would be swimming in moonlight: the great yellow allamanda, the love vine climbing the stairs, the fleshy hibiscus where sun birds dipped at noon. I was beginning to know the names. But for the faceless creature within, old touch-me-not, whose every stir of elbow or knee I felt as immediately and blindly as my own heartbeat, I had no name. Nor wished to. That would have been to acknowledge as permanent the eclipse of the only self I had ever known, a self that prided itself on refusing to take part. It was the dazed shame of defeat I felt, lying there watching the moonlight. I had seen the wise nods of the old women, the attempted embrace of the mothers. Now you'll see, I read in the press of their lips. Oh no, I wanted to answer, there you're mistaken. Don't suppose that because of this I have become like you, trapped in body and soul.

By day, my body swelling before the curious gaze of the schoolboys we taught. There was Lamikanra whose mother came down from Abeokuta every week with the school's supply of eggs, Ogedegbe, and Kpaduwa. Umenne who would go to Moscow to study engineering, and the beautiful Binitie. Plato Syrimis, son of a Greek father, the school's tennis champion, and little Olatunbosun. The smiling Ogundele who, it was said, when he was eight had tried to throw himself down the village well; and Davies, bundled in a woolen scarf at the first sign of rain, treating himself for catarrh. There was Okorie, his cheeks deeply grooved with tribal markings, who had memorized the whole of act 3 of *Macbeth*. And Johnson, his friend, an albino with tight red hair. For a time, Oridota, whom we privately called Alyosha because he had the calm and limpid eyes of Alexey Karamazov. And Sobomowo, taller than the others, his forehead knit into a permanent frown of earnestness and longing. They sat at desks in classrooms open on one side to a view of the path that led to our house and to the enormous grapefruit tree whose fruit we ate, pink in a thick chalky rind. Classrooms open to stepping hens and to lizards that scuttled in and froze, legs pumping, before rushing out again into the sun. The boys liked lists of words: poetry, of whatever kind, to be memorized and turned in the mouth. But always the preference was for Shakespeare with his witches and kings and yellow stockings, cross-gartered, with his pelting nights and fools.

The boys handed in notebooks with the Igbobi College insignia printed on the cover, and when the pile on my desk was complete a boy always asked if he could carry it for me back to the house. To this I said yes. But in response to their quick courtesy, would I like a seat, take this one, I feigned distraction. Brushing the suggestion aside as if I hadn't heard, as if it had nothing to do with anything, I tilted on the desk, balanced my bulk with a sandal on the cement floor.

Again, the dumb incomprehension, the idiot gaze, when the Polish doctor in his office on Ikorodu Road asked questions. Was I careful to eat well? Had the baby begun to move? One side of his face was stained by a strawberry mark; it fell down his cheek in the shape of a drop, like the melancholy slash beneath the eyes of clowns. The walls of his office were covered with glass cases holding mounted butterflies. In the half-light of the shuttered room, the fan revolving slowly overhead, wings spread everywhere poised for flight. Wings beating wildly, deathly afraid. Oh yes, eating well. But in response to the other question, silence. A flutter within, unrecognizable. Just behind his head was a case with two butterflies pinned side by side. One set of wings was pale green, tapered narrowly at the ends like bits of tattered silk. The other was the color of lapis lazuli. To have pronounced the word, *baby*, would have been to admit openly that there was no way back, no way to invite the return of the lightdazzle self so recently betrayed.

Then the women sitting in the corridor outside Dr. Odianju's office at the Lagos Island Maternity Hospital.

Obediently waiting on two long rows of benches, we faced each other across the little loaves rising in us like tomorrow's lunch. Absurd, all of us herded together like that, a flock of swollen sheep. We were not to make an objection or to speak out of turn. Every few minutes Dr. Odianju came to the door of his office and read out a name. A woman got up, adjusted the cloth worn high and smooth beneath her breasts, and made her careful way down the aisle of busy wombs. She balanced her freight narrowly, tilting first to one side then to the other, so as not to topple headlong, disgraced.

Three days after Zara was born, I held her in one arm outside the elevator in the hospital and looked into her face. It escaped me completely. The veined eyelids were sealed tight as gum. A knuckle, a turtle dreaming in its shell, a pale round pearl, remote and entire. Left to myself I could contemplate the stunning aloofness of this creature without misgivings. But when people looked at Zara asleep in my arms, at her tiny body slung over my shoulder, their faces went slack with approval. There was nothing to be said except that they were wrong, mistaken in what they thought they saw.

What did I know except that I was not a mother? Only later did I understand it is not immediate, not what is called natural, the taking to oneself of a child. It is a discipline learned slowly and painfully, a discipline for which it is always too late: the arm that bends comfortably to the body straining at the same time for comfort and escape, the hands that caress but do not detain.

And now, visiting Zara, the guest of her house, I am again unsure what to do. The day after my arrival I tell her she must sometimes go out and see her friends without me, just as she would if I were not here. She must do this soon so that we do not get into a habit of going everywhere together. What I do not say is that I do not want her to feel constrained by my presence. I know a mother visiting a grown child should be careful not to get in the way, should make herself scarce. And for the first time I understand the fierce desire for independence of the elderly, the need to maintain a roof of their own. As the guest of one's child, discreet, accommodating, one has become again the mother who lives to the rhythms of that other creature, the child of one's womb. And a child, sheltering her mother, may be driven by affection, generosity, the desire to share everything she has, but is helpless to forget the unappeased longing, the hunger in the night that her mother's breasts only so partially satisfied.

Walking down the street in Matameye, alone, I hear "*Sannu*, Mama," or sometimes, "*Sannu*, Madame Zara." As when Zara was hidden within, herself stark and sexless, so I have become once again an abstraction, something remote and shapeless, a stranger in disguise.

Full Moon

Ba ɗon tsawo a kan ga wata ba.
It is not because we are tall that we see the moon.

One night we close the gate behind us, on our way to visit Maimoun. A full moon is rising over the walls of Matameye, bone white and immense; a moon with a face tipped in woe, in helpless grief for things to come. Behind, the sky falls into further and further reaches of blue, the air so pure it seems another form of light. On the sand the shadows are long and solemn. We step in and out of them, nonchalant, pretending to ignore the moon. With nightfall, Matameye has at last become itself: one enormous, partitioned room where footsteps are muffled by sand, and the ceiling is the sky. From behind the walls, voices murmur and drift, the intimate sounds of night visiting. In the street, along the walls, people are sitting on mats, their children stretched beside them. Others, like ourselves, are on their way somewhere, and softly exchange a greeting as they pass. Inside a little boutique a kerosene lantern makes a golden display of jars of pomade, Rothman cigarettes, cones of sugar wrapped in blue paper.

We want nothing tonight. Zara is telling me in a hushed,

excited voice about the trip she made with two friends to Nguigmi last Christmas, about the sand dune they climbed at sunset, feet sinking back half a step for every step they climbed. Fifty feet high, and at the top—here Zara stops short, arrested by the vision she is describing—they had looked out for miles into a crystal stillness of sand and scrubby bush. As they watched, the shadows cast by the dunes began slowly, scarcely perceptibly, to undulate. Then, when it was almost dark, Zara and her friends had rolled over and over down the wall of soft sand. The next morning it was all gone, the landscape had entirely shifted; there was nothing to recognize.

A tailor is bent late over his sewing machine, the glow of the lantern beside him reaching into the corners of his shop. Yesterday afternoon, when we passed, a group of children were sitting barefoot on mats, writing on their wooden scrolls. The tailor is a *malam* and conducts a Qur'anic school, but then as now he was at his machine, the silver wheel humming. Zara has told me that he embroiders the shirts we can see hanging at the back of the shop. His work is intricate, surpassing, and when people need something to wear for *Salla* or a wedding, they come to him. He seems to listen carefully to whatever it is they say they want, but when they return to collect their new clothes they are always astonished. What has he done, embroidering a crescent moon into a length of sleeve, using blue thread instead of gold? Or cutting the neck in fanciful scallops? Some are angry and refuse to pay, others are delighted. But even the baffled ones come back. Now, despite the moon, his eyes are on the task at hand, his foot steadily pumping the treadle.

We turn one corner and then another and another. Already the moon is floating free of the walls, spilling light on every face. Zara is telling me another desert story from the same trip, about the nuns they met outside Nguigmi, an Italian and a Dutch woman, living in a tent. They belonged to a

European religious order that lives with nomads and for the last years they had been traveling with Toubous, a group that moves with herds around the shores of Lake Chad. Each nun had her own goats, made her own mats and skin pouches, and pounded the millet she ate. The Dutch sister, Ria, had once traveled with Gypsies in Spain and she told stories late into the night. They had all sat around a fire at the foot of a dune, roasting potatoes and drinking Tuareg tea. Zara is describing how a boy on a camel had suddenly appeared out of nowhere, from the deep silence on the far side of the dune, when she and I turn a corner and all at once are facing an open field of sand soaked in light.

There is a wall at one end, cut up and down with doorways deep in shadow. Outside, lying on mats, people are waiting for the air to cool. We cross the sand, shadows dipping in front of us, but stop once to turn and look back at the moon, higher now, its face still pocked with seas of foreboding. Then we are facing Maimoun's door, and Zara leans over and claps her hands softly in front of her thighs: "*Salamu Alaikum,*" she calls. In a moment Maimoun is in the *zaure:* "*Alaiku salamu,*" she says. "*Sannu ∂a zuwa, sannu.*" And then she breaks into a soft laugh, embarrassed, teasing. She is a tall woman with a baby on her back and a quick, sidelong glance. Neither Maimoun nor I make any gesture of surprise. We are both aware Zara has described us to the other and are discreet in our approach. Leaving our sandals behind, Zara and I follow her through the doorway into the darkness of the enclosed *zaure* and out into the clear light of the open court.

The children are awake. They are jumping up and down in front of a wall, throwing out their arms and legs to make shadows. When we walk in they are still, and the little girl dips to her knee, a complete curtsy. This is Biba, and the smaller boy is Cezali. He walks to Maimoun's side and takes her hand, then looks at me eagerly. Zara is familiar to him, but

I am not, and Maimoun, pointing from me to Zara, explains that this is Zara's mother. My blue eyes are frightening, this I know, much more frightening than the novelty of white skin, and Zara's eyes are dark. The older boy, Nahiou, stands in the doorway of the room off the court, half in, half out. His shoulder is turned toward us, his head lowered, and he is looking at us with quick glances. Maimoun says that Sani has just come in from their millet fields, a three-hour walk south of Matameye, where he has been working for the past several days. He returned only a few minutes ago and is now inside washing. In a moment he dips through the door where Nahiou is standing and, lightly tapping his chest with a loose fist, bowing, welcomes us.

Maimoun has long eyes, tilting upward at the corners. She looks at me aslant while bending to reassure Cezali, explaining Sani's whereabouts. She and Zara, standing side by side when Sani enters, take hands and swing them back and forth loosely for a moment before letting go.

There is a little neem tree in the middle of the court, barely higher than our heads, throwing a shadow across the sand and up a wall. In one corner, a black iron pot sits on a ring of stones. It is surrounded by several enamel *kwanos,* some with lids, some without, a silver dipper, and by the *tukunya,* a large clay pot where the water is kept cool. The children had been almost asleep, Maimoun says, turning to me, but when Sani came in they woke up and began to play. Now she tells them to lie down again, and Nahiou and Biba first sit cross-legged and finally sprawl on the mattress next to the wall, Cezali on the mat beside it. They are lying still but wide awake to the moon watching us from above the wall of the court, pouring light everywhere.

As the guest, I am to sit in the single chair under the neem tree, Maimoun and Zara on a mat across from me. Sani disappears into the room for a moment but, when he returns, squats at a little distance from us on a wooden stool. Then the formal greetings begin, the questions, the answering note of reassurance and embrace. The baby is well, thanks be to Allah, my long trip has been a safe one, Sani's weariness is nothing. A lengthening hum of silence separates the final questions, then there is a pause that opens to ordinary talk.

The *hatsi*—the millet—is this high, Sani says, and he extends a hand to show us, a foot from the ground. Sani has a reflective face, drawn with fatigue. He turns his palm up, shrugs, and lets it drop next to his side.

By now the millet should be further along. Unless the plant matures enough to produce the tight cone in which the seed nestles, it is useless, worth nothing more than the stalks and leaves from which mats and the walls of huts are woven. At best, there is rain enough in Matameye for only one millet cycle. A little further to the south, around Kano, there may sometimes be enough for two. Yet it is not so much the lack of rain this year, Sani continues, but the sandstorm about a month ago that bowed the new plants to the ground. Maimoun and Zara nod, yes, who could forget, at two o'clock in the afternoon the sky was black as night. You couldn't see six inches in front of your face. Maimoun says her mother remembered something like it as a child, but she herself, never, that people who were outside at the time had simply fallen to the ground, covering their heads.

He was on his way out to the millet fields, Sani continues, elbows resting on his knees, he had just reached the plots they were leaving fallow this year, when a wind sprang up that almost knocked him off his feet. Then it was dark, nothing but sand. He had crouched by the side of the road, arms over his face, not daring to move. For some time he had remained like that, listening to the hiss and roar, when he heard someone crying. He had opened his eyes just long enough to see a couple of Fulani children, maybe Nahiou's age, seven or eight, running up and down, hands pressed against their faces, pointed linen caps pulled down low over their ears. Their goats were with them. Then they were all gone, the sand had swept them away, and when he called out he heard nothing.

At this Cezali, eyes wide, gets up from the mat where he is lying and comes to stand in front of his father. Sani speaks to him in a low voice, and Cezali moves forward, a little at a time, until he is standing between his father's knees. Their faces are at a level; we can hear only the continuing murmur of Sani's voice. After a few minutes Cezali lies down again, and in a moment his chest is rising and falling in the deep breath of sleep. Sani gets up from the stool, saying he's glad to be back in town and is going to sit for a while outside the wall. He nods to us and disappears through the *zaure*.

As soon as he is gone, Maimoun begins to tell us how three beggars had taken refuge in the *zaure* during the sandstorm, how they had stepped inside and stayed there until it had passed. The baby, Fasuma, has been making small grunting noises for the last minutes, and Maimoun, still speaking, reaches back with one arm and pulls her forward, at the same time lifting her blouse to uncover her breast.

The beggars were three blind old women led by a little girl, Maimoun says, easing Fasuma into the crook of her arm and settling the breast in her mouth, and the old women's dark shawls were blowing over their faces. Cezali had said to Biba that if the beggars saw her they would try to steal her eyes. Biba had been terrified and had tried to flatten herself against the wall. She refused to move or to speak. Then Nahiou had asked how Cezali thought that beggars who were blind could steal anyone's eyes. How would they be able to see the eyes in order to snatch them?

But it didn't matter; since that time Biba has been having bad dreams. We look at her now, curled in on herself, her back pressed along one of Nahiou's legs. The boys' hair is cut close to their heads. Biba's is braided in neat cornrows and wound at the ends with string.

"Did you know, Maimoun," Zara asks, "that El Gouni's daughter—you know, Marianma—is coming to Matameye soon to visit her?"

Zara has told me already that El Gouni remembers Maimoun as a little girl, that Marianma is a few years older than Maimoun but that as children they used to play together.

Maimoun says yes, that yesterday she had seen El Gouni, who told her so. She will be glad to see Marianma, she says; she has suffered very much.

But Maimoun is preoccupied, is slowly rubbing her wrist back and forth across the breast still waiting for Fasuma, a gesture like a sleepy child's rubbing her eyes: this, I know, to keep back the flow of milk. Fasuma, at the other breast, is drinking greedily, swallowing with noisy gulps. Her eyes are rolling up beneath the lids in delirium. Sweat is breaking out on her forehead. Around her neck is a string of amulets and the tiny bottoms of her feet are hennaed. She is sprawled across Maimoun's lap, one hand closed tight around Maimoun's finger, the other open and slapping the breast. Maimoun and Zara and I are watching her, transfixed. *Yarinya,* Zara says, leaning forward to touch one of her heels. Aren't you hurting your mother, hitting her like that?

Maimoun looks at me, and we exchange a smile—intimate, fleeting—that excludes Zara. We are demonstrating our mutual love for her by taking this opportunity to establish some understanding of our own, but we are also mothers exercising a smug sense of privilege in the company of a woman who is not a mother. This is another version of the knowing smile I had hated before Zara was born. At that time I had seen in it only the grimace of defeated mothers at last triumphant before the daughters they had envied: now you'll see what I've been telling you all along, how changed life is when you have to think of someone besides yourself. Tonight I know it also acknowledges a wordless bonding in the flesh, a consorority of secret pleasures.

It is by Zara's next question that I suppose she has observed our complicity. "And Talatuwa?" she asks Maimoun. "Did you see her today?"

Maimoun and Zara are sitting side by side on the mat beneath the neem tree. The moon is moving up through the branches, the court is flooded with light. Maimoun shifts Fasuma to the other breast and with the long fingers of one hand encircles her tiny knee. Talatuwa the firstborn, child of *koumia*, child of shame, disowned in the midst of all this complacent maternity.

Maimoun shakes her head slowly. "*A'a*," she says. No, in Hausa, the second syllable four tones lower than the first. She glances down to meet Fasuma's stare, nodding and lifting her eyebrows in greeting. Fasuma kicks her feet, her mouth stops its busy sucking. Her gaze is rapt. When Maimoun again raises her eyes to us, Fasuma watches her as intently as before.

"But I had such a strange dream last night," Maimoun tells us. "I remembered it only this moment." Then she says that in the dream she was coming through the *zaure* and stumbled over a baby, a baby she recognized from some distant time. When she saw this baby lying on the floor, a mere scrap of a thing, naked, without a cloth or dress, without a bracelet for her ankle or wrist, she had wept bitter tears. She had snatched up the baby, clasping it to her, but the baby was immediately transformed into a ten-year-old girl with budding breasts, a young girl who walked out of the *zaure* into the noonday sun without looking back.

Zara makes a hum of assent, and Maimoun lowers her

head. We can see the elaborate pattern of braids that wraps it, circles that fit one inside another narrowing to a point high on her skull. Then she looks up suddenly, dropping her hand onto Zara's thigh, looking first into my eyes, then into Zara's. "I thought it was Talatuwa," she says, "and when I woke my heart was sad."

Zara clasps Maimoun's hand in sympathy, holds it in her own. She plays with Maimoun's fingers, twisting a ring that she is wearing on her middle finger, tracing the henna spot in the middle of her palm. And although I can remember Lizzy and Tulu, when they were little, turning a ring on my hand, lifting each of my fingers and letting it drop, slapping their palms against mine, I have no recollection of Zara ever doing the same. To avoid breaking in, of again establishing a link with Maimoun that excludes Zara, or perhaps out of sheer embarrassment that Zara should hear me say such a thing, I do not confess that I, too, have had dreams similar to Maimoun's.

Then, in a flash, I understand that it is in my dreams, in my unwilling recognitions, that I am discovering how deeply familiar Matameye is to me. What I know of Matameye is Zara herself, my feelings for her. And I wonder now, with mild surprise, that so recently this world had seemed to contain nothing recognizable.

But Fasuma's eyes are closing, her mouth is going slack. Every now and then she draws a long convulsive breath, then settles more deeply in sleep. *Sarkin barci,* Maimoun murmurs: chief of sleep. When Fasuma is completely still, Maimoun lays her in Zara's lap, saying as she gets up she wants to put a cloth under the mat where Cezali is sleeping, the sand makes a hard bed. After she has lifted him by a wrist and an ankle and placed him on the mattress, she folds a *pagne,* lays it flat under the mat where he was sleeping, and lifts him back again. Suddenly he sits straight up, eyes wide open, and stares at us from the depths of his sleep. Behind his small figure a shadow shoots up the wall. He looks at us without blinking, moon globes reflected in his dark eyes. A moment later, he falls backward onto the mat, extinguished.

Sani has come in carrying the mottled plastic kettle used for ablutions. He disappears into the room off the court and a few minutes later passes with his goat skin, his prayer mat: he is going out again to say his prayers. It is time for us to leave. Maimoun prepares to accompany us, at least part of the way. She centers Fasuma in the middle of her back, covering her with a *pagne*, straightens, and lifts another *pagne* over her own head. We slip on our sandals, dip through the *zaure*—where the children's wooden scrolls are leaning in a corner and where Maimoun so recently encountered the ghost of her child—and are out again, on the other side of the wall. The moon is high; it is faceless now, no longer leaning above the world in commiseration and sorrow. Looking back, we can see Sani standing at the edge of the goat's skin, staring straight ahead. A moment later he is bent double, hands on his knees, in *ruku:* "My ears, my eyes, my brain, my bones, my tendons and whatever else is carried by my feet, all is submitted to Allah."

My own mother's prayer, something like it, on her deathbed, when her bones could be numbered one by one. When she had become too wasted to eat her bread; when tears mingled with her drink.

But now Maimoun is telling us that when she was a child, this long dip where we are walking was a pond during the rainy season. In fact, Matameye used to be full of ponds; it is a village said to have been built on springs. We can hear the frogs from somewhere in the distance, in the seep of some moist place, and can hear drums, too, a sound familiar at any time of the day or night. She says that when she and Marianma were children they used to plunge their arms into the sand as deep as they would go, and sometimes, depending on the season, their fingers would touch water. That was before the drought had occurred. It would be impossible to do that today.

Then she says something rapidly to Zara that I don't understand. Zara tells me Maimoun is asking if I knew that the word *matameye* means "the women have conquered." The legend is that a woman founded the village, and that years later her twin brother came along and took it away from her. After that, the rains stopped falling and the wells dried up. Women's breasts no longer ran with milk.

We pass people at little tables outside their walls, some talking, some sitting silently in the moonlight. Children are sleeping on mats at their parents' feet. In the middle of our path, lying on their stomachs in the sand, two boys are talking softly, their outstretched legs, pointing in opposite directions, making a single straight line. Chins in their palms, these friends are lost to everything. We step around their legs in silence, keeping a respectful distance.

Then, when we are past, Maimoun tells us something else she remembers, how when she was much younger than that—she gestures with her chin behind us toward the boys—her father sometimes carried her home at night. He carried her on his arm, and as they walked along she looked over his shoulder and thought the moon was following them. When they stopped to talk to someone, she thought the moon had stopped too, waiting, and that it would begin to move again when they did. Recently she told her father about this and he said she was much too young at the time to remember. But she did remember, she told him, she remembered very well.

We are halfway to Zara's compound and Maimoun is going to return home. She lifts a hand to say goodbye: on her palm the hennaed dot, black on amber. We exchange greetings and she moves away, head covered, Fasuma's bulge riding the middle of her back.

Zara and I resume our path between walls overhung with neem branches that make dark patches on the sand beneath. Our own shadows are brief, moving side by side. In another direction, away from us, Maimoun is walking alone.

"I was sorry to miss Talatuwa," I say after a few moments.

"Well, that's the way it is," Zara answers. "She comes and goes. I'm always a little uneasy when she's around. It's so striking, the difference in the way Maimoun treats her and the others."

Zara's face is clear in the moonlight. In one of her hands she is carrying the little black leather change purse from which she took the coin Deje refused for her groundnuts on the night of the new moon.

"When Maimoun told us her dream, though, you seemed very sympathetic," I say. "I mean, the way you reached out for her hand."

"Oh yes, I know Maimoun suffers too. I can see that when Talatuwa visits. Maimoun has outbursts, sometimes, that leave her miserable afterward."

Easy for me to imagine: it might be the bowl slipping from unsure hands, the chop of her cough, and there it would be again, the sudden sob that rises to the throat in harshness, the reproach that builds a wall against the surging tide of grief. Anger masking the fear that there will be no recovery from a loss as severe as this one.

"As for holding her hand," Zara continues, turning to me earnestly, "it's one of the things I like best about being here, the easy way people touch each other all the time—you've seen how it is—holding hands walking down the street, sitting around talking."

At the corner, where the walls on either side of us diverge, a *gawo* tree rises abruptly from the sand, its branches full of roosting peacocks. Their tails hang in dark wisps, but their backs are sleek and silver.

"You know, Zara," I say, taking courage from the dark tree, from the peacocks shimmering beneath the moon, "when you were little I don't remember your sitting on my lap much. That kind of thing."

As if Zara's thoughts were running of themselves in the same direction, she answers immediately. "No," she says. "I don't either. Holding your hand when we went out, yes. But the rest, not so much. I remember Lizzy and Tulu doing more of that." She laughs, a strained laugh, painful to hear. "You know, the firstborn," she says.

Then, abruptly changing the subject, she tells me there's another advantage for them all, running along completely different lines, in Talatuwa's living with her grandmother. "Things are scarce," she says. "They have what they get from the millet crop, and then what Sani can make during the dry season, repairing watches. Even for *Salla*, they didn't have goat's meat. The children are thinner than they were a few months ago."

We are almost home, passing the corner where the tailor was bent over his sewing machine. But now his stand is dark. In front of it an old woman who wasn't there earlier is sitting on a mat. "*Sannu, Tsohuwa*," Zara calls out as we pass, and the woman inclines her head. Her cheekbones are high and raw, the planes beneath are dark. Above one elbow she is wearing a silver bracelet. *Tsohuwa:* old woman. *Mace:* woman. *Yarinya:* little girl. Zara is explaining the difference in how the words are used, when we push open the gate of the compound to find the moon everywhere over the face of the little house. There is a silver sheen on the tin roof. It is much too bright to go inside right away, so we sit down in the string chairs, our feet drawn up on the top rungs. The shadow of the neem runs along the cement floor where we are sitting and, in a smooth drop, like water, down onto the sand.

"The old woman we just passed. Did you notice her?"

Zara asks. She is leaning back in her chair, hands folded together behind her head.

I say that I did.

"Maimoun told me about her once," Zara says, looking up into the sky, "and since then other people have pointed her out to me."

While the night expands around us, Zara tells me the story, how a long time ago the old woman was married to the wealthiest man in Matameye, the father of El Hadji who brought the peacocks here. He was said to be the wealthiest man and she the most beautiful woman. That is what people called her: the most beautiful woman in Matameye. In any case, one day she decided she'd had enough of lying against embroidered pillows and left her husband's compound to sit on a mat outside the wall. She sold matches. Everyone was scandalized, her husband begged her to return, but she was adamant. She preferred the street, she said. Her husband offered inducements of every kind, a trip to Mecca, a trip, in fact, wherever she wanted to go. She said it wasn't worth it to her, she preferred moving around with her mat. For a long time her husband pursued her—with threats after the promises wore out—but she never went back. He has been dead now a long time, but people say that during the last years, when he passed her on the street, sitting with her matches, he would bow from the waist. No one knew if he was doing this to mock her, or if he meant it as some kind of tribute.

"But there she is still," Zara says, as if she were reciting the end of a fairy tale, "doing as she wishes."

We sit for a while, thinking about that, and then I ask Zara what about Sani, how did Maimoun come to marry him. "She was thirteen and in love with somebody else," Zara says. "But Sani spoke to her father; he was older, considered a good match, and it was arranged. They're content, I think, but the difference is that Sani chose her and she didn't choose him. That's felt between them. And he's never taken another wife. Maimoun says sometimes she wishes he would, to help with the work. But if it came to it, I'm not so sure."

I ask if this is the way it's usually done, with the father deciding.

"Well, sometimes," Zara answers, hesitating, choosing her words, "but not always. Not by any means. Sometimes people choose each other. And sometimes spectacular things happen."

And she tells me about Koubra, Maimoun's sister, who was in love with a man named Rabi. The father insisted, as he had done with Maimoun, that she marry someone else, the suitor he had chosen. She obeyed. But after the first night with the new husband, she left him, saying she'd had enough. She went straight to Kantché, to the seat of the powerful Chef de Canton, and begged him to annul the marriage. Under no circumstances, she said, would she live with this man. Her father was shamed, he pleaded with her to return. But to the surprise of everyone the *sarki* gave her what she wanted. He annulled the marriage, and she and Rabi were married immediately. They have a very different kind of marriage from Maimoun's and Sani's. They fight and make up and for a while are ecstatically happy, then they fight again.

"You know them too?" I ask.

"Oh yes," Zara says, stretching her legs out in front of her, then slowly rising to her feet. "Maimoun and Koubra spend a lot of time together. In fact, Koubra had a baby boy the same week that Fasuma was born, but he never started breathing. They said his heart wasn't functioning properly. Koubra was very subdued afterward. She kept saying over and over that when she saw him lying there so quietly she thought he was sleeping. In the midst of celebrating Fasuma's birth, we were all very sad. And Rabi had already bought the fat baptismal ram. I saw it standing in their compound when I went over to give my condolences. At least the ram was pleased with the turn of events. He held his curly horns high."

After Zara goes inside I sit for a while longer in the night. I am thinking how the greetings we exchanged with Maimoun, then with Sani, go on all day long and late into the night. It is impossible to pass someone in the street in silence, to begin a conversation with Maimoun without asking the same questions put to a stranger. Several times a day each person in Matameye reminds others, and is reminded in turn, that all life hangs on the certain journey of the sun across the sky and the highly uncertain fall of rain, that work is a gift for which thanks must be given, that blood relations may be expected to answer for one another, and that peace of heart is acquired through the long practice of patience. The questions may vary, Zara tells me, according to the time of day or the season of the year. But the response is always the same. No, there isn't any fatigue, although it was clear Sani was dropping from it. The children are well. Sleep has restored. It's not this moment that matters, it seems, and how one is placed in it. Rather it's that every life, secure in the infinite embrace of Allah, is touched by hunger, death, and sleepless nights. What matters is continuity, the things that bind one generation to another, whatever remains after the worst has been done. One person is saluting another on the bare fact of the humanity they share: irreducible, fraught with danger, and for this moment, survived.

The moon is high, now, small in a sky of dissolving blue. Its light is streaming everywhere, down the sides of the neem trees, over the rounded tops of the walls. Maimoun, by now, must have finished saying her prayers. And Koubra? Is she at this moment holding Rabi, her back arched in delight? And later on, when the moon is fading in the west, when the peacocks are stirring in the *gawo* trees, will she be dreaming of her lost child, the one whose sleep had seemed to her the mark of its perfection?

Labarin zuciya a tambayi fuska.
For news of the heart consult the face.

One morning, early, it's not Zara but myself who sits alone with her feet up, drinking coffee from a plastic turquoise mug. It rained last night and the sand is still damp in spots, ruddy brown drying to gold. On the roof a dove is softly cooing and from everywhere, in the branches, along the walls, the twitter of Senegalese fire finches rises against the cries of vendors passing in the street beyond the gate. First comes the call of the woman selling *hura:* a nasal slur, plaintive, breaking off in the air; and a few minutes later the sliding notes of the boy who carries water in the kerosene cans that swing from the halter cradling his neck. On all sides there is a freshness this morning, a rustling cool. At the foot of the wall a female lizard is digging the hole where she will lay her eggs. She burrows with her dusty head, then scrapes away the loose sand, her tiny foot curled in like a cat's paw.

A breeze is blowing the tops of the neem trees, tossing the leaves. In the next compound the whish of El Gouni's broom scrapes and pauses. She is tidying up her compound, perhaps thinking of Marianma's approaching visit as she works, gathering into piles the leaves that came down with last night's rain; like everyone sweeping this morning she is etching a new pattern of moons in the sand: a row of cusps pointing one way, then, when she turns at the wall, another row, counter. By noon these strokes, vivid now, will have been obliterated by light. Later again, in the course of the long afternoon, they will begin to move across the sand like waves.

It is still very early, but Zara is out fetching the vaccines from the refrigerator at the Centre Medical. Today we are going to Kantché, as she does one day every week, about fifteen kilometers north of Matameye on the road to Takieta, at which point it joins the Route Nationale and becomes the road to Zinder. There is no electricity in Kantché, so Zara will carry the vaccines in a little box packed with ice. Last night she boiled syringes in a pan and put them in the sack that hangs from behind the seat of her mobylette. She also borrowed a mobylette for me, along with a yellow globe helmet like her own. In Kantché there is a small clinic, built only a few years ago, but for generations this village has been the seat of the *sarki* of the region, now called the Chef de Canton. When he rides with his courtiers into Matameye on a horse caparisoned in cloth of gold, men and women drop to their knees. It is to him that Maimoun's sister, Koubra, applied when she left her husband of one night. But he is known to the larger world as well. When Hamani Diori was president, the Chef de Canton served as one of his ministers and after the coup was the only member of the government to escape imprisonment: a tribute, perhaps, to his incorruptible honor. Maimoun told Zara that wherever he goes his old aunt travels with him because she alone can prepare *bura* to suit his taste.

When Zara returns, she fits the vaccines alongside the syringes and fastens the buckle of the case. Then she shows me how to jump start the bike I will ride, how to turn the handgrips inward for speed, outward to brake, and we are off, she leading the way, down the sandy streets of Matameye and out. At the edge of town we speed past the market, the *auto gare*, and the cinder-block school where girls in green skirts and white blouses are jumping rope, then onto the paved road the *taxi brousse* followed a couple of weeks ago on its slow way to Zinder. The road is planted on either side with neem trees and their branches throw dim morning shadows across the tar still wet in places from last night's rain. Today is Friday, market day, and people are coming into town, moving under the trees while the sun is still low in the sky. We pass a boy driving a donkey piled with wood, and behind him three Fulani women striding along in white plastic shoes, heads poised beneath nests of calabashes tied in a net. On the other side of the road, a man trots lightly toward us on a black horse. He is wearing a white turban and the cloth beneath his saddle is closely embroidered in green, red, and orange. The horse prances by and then there is a little girl with a tray of *goro*, kola nuts, on her head, walking beside an old man on a donkey. The old man is seated far back, almost hidden behind a flapping mass of leafy branches. Each one we pass, even a man carrying a sewing machine on his head, lifts a hand in greeting. After a few moments of clinging fearfully to the handlebars, I do the same.

Bikes tilted, we follow the curve in the road that leaves Matameye behind and have just begun to pull upright when, to our left, we are looking down into a grove of palm trees. It could be an apparition, these palms sprouting energetically in the sands of Niger, and beneath them millet plants, already tightly coned and ready for harvest. In fact it is an alluvial basin, an oasis, referred to by name in Matameye. Then it has whirled away beneath us, and we are out on the broad road, looking across a distance so immense it provokes a kind of vertigo. Space turning on its axis. There is the land, a flat expanse of it sweeping further and further away until it disappears with the curve of the earth; and there is the sky. But the sky is so vast above our heads, so still, it seems if we let go for an instant we might fall into it. A flock of egrets wheels and turns, a flash of white.

We are careful to look down, to keep the mobylettes on the tarred road, avoiding the sand that spins by close to the wheels, careful to glance backward for a *camion* or *taxi brousse* creeping up from behind. Zara's heels in her flip-flops are pink, turned inward toward the buzzing motor of her bike, exposed to the hurtling road beneath. We pass a man leading a camel by a rope. He lifts a hand, but after he is gone something remains of robes fluttering around slender legs, a camel drifting reluctantly behind, nostrils in the air.

Then, as before, there is only land and sky. But now each is assuming form and color. The sky is mollusked white and silver after last night's rain. It is a cool sky, shot like silk with sudden gleams and ripples. Beneath, soil finds its level in sand, baobabs and spiky acacia here and there piercing the long overflow. The baobabs erupt suddenly, trunks smooth, branches flung to the sky. Even from a distance we can see their pale green pods tossing in the wind. There are *gawo* trees as well, lacy with thorns, turning in the silver light. And then, here and there, unbidden, plots of millet slowly rise to the sheltered plane of our sight, green plants wet and shining against the rusty earth. The stalks are only a few inches out of the ground. But the leaves that will spread to allow the grain are already pointing toward the sun. Solitary in the space laid out before us, a man reaches with a long-handled hoe, bends, straightens. Then he is gone and a woman takes his place, again solitary, lost in the endless flux of sand and tree.

From beneath an acacia bush close to the road, a pied crow rises with a stern flap flap of great black wings; it swerves and is lost behind us. And now, moving across the horizon, is a village, the cone roofs of its huts rising in points above the golden meshed wall that encircles it. A woman is walking away from the village, a shiny brown gourd on her head. She crosses in front of a cluster of granaries and disappears. The village, too, passes slowly from sight, and then again, on every side, there is only the immense reach of land, extending flat in every direction until we can see no further. In the east the silver disk of the sun slides from behind a cloud. From out of the scrub, released by last night's rain, field after field of millet opens to meet it, the delicate green of the leaves washed clean and vivid. A boy in a tunic is bent over the plants. He chops at the soil with a short hoe and is gone. In the distance, there is another village and near it a man driving a team of white oxen. He guides the rudder of the plow between the laboring animals. And then, again, only the endless fling of land and bush. On either side of us the horizon is so wide and so still that our small, individual speed is reduced to nothing. This is the face of the earth and we are passing over it. For once, time has given way to the buoyancies of space, and with it all fear of falling, all anxiety for the future, has vanished in a landscape of perfect visibility.

We know we are approaching Kantché when we see a man walking toward us, arms hooked over the long-handled hoe resting on his neck and shoulders. Crosstree on a mast, a figure hanging on a rood. Behind him is another man, also carrying a hoe, and a boy pulling a cart with rubber wheels. There are women too, some walking by themselves, others in a line, but they carry their hoes against one shoulder, the scything metal blade riding in front. We are going more slowly now and pass a little girl with a baby on her back. She lifts her hand, turning her head as we pass, and disappears. Then there is a young man jogging along on the rump of a donkey, bags of millet in front, and beside the road a stork stepping in a pool beneath a mango tree. It lowers its beak and throws back the long tube of its neck. The signpost for Kantché comes rushing forward, blue block letters on a white background, and we break our speed to a putter, avoiding the herd of goats trotting delicately in the middle of the road. We veer west into the town itself, down narrow sandy aisles bordered on either side by houses with slender minarets. Over their doorways, already deep in shadow, are the intersecting rectangles and loops familiar from the old town of Zinder. These houses, too, have high embrasured windows, narrow on the face of the *zaures,* and wooden drainpipes jutting from the roofs.

We approach the *dispensaire* from behind, plowing a path through open banks of sand that finally are too deep for the mobylettes. When we can no longer keep our balance, we get off and push.

The *dispensaire* is a low cement building with a large red cross painted over the entrance; on the steps running its length women sit with babies in their laps, waving straw fans slowly back and forth to keep away the flies. Children are climbing up and down the steps on short legs or leaning against their mothers, watching. At one end, a young woman wearing a white lab coat over her *pagne,* hair smoothed into a knot at the back of her head, sits with a cloth book held up in front of her. She is talking loudly to the other women, but when we are near she gets up and comes across the sand to greet us, throwing one leg out at the hip, sinking with the other in the sand.

This is Amina, whom Zara has told me is lame from an injection that hit the sciatic nerve when she was a child. She extends her hand, which Zara catches in her own, and they stand there, side by side, two young women in *pagnes* wrapped around their hips, while Amina sings out a brisk *"Bon jour, Mama. Ça va?"* Her eyes are both canny and caressing; they linger on my face without embarrassment and I have to remind myself not to look away. Then Zara, relinquishing Amina's hand, goes inside to prepare the syringes and I sit down on the step while Amina finishes her lesson.

Because of last night's rain, only a few women have come to the clinic this morning. The others are in the fields. Amina is holding up a picture of a mournful child squatting in the sand, a thin stream of diarrhea running from its buttocks. Beside it is a tree whose leaves hang lifeless from drooping branches. Amina is saying that a child with diarrhea is like a tree that is suffering from lack of rain. Both have lost the fluids necessary for health. She points to the child, then to the tree, and back again to the child. The child is sick; what the child needs is water. Amina lifts the cloth page and underneath it is another picture, this time of a woman with a smiling baby on her lap, holding a cup of water to the baby's mouth. Next to them is a tree with rain falling on it, its leafy branches held high.

Amina asks the women why the child is feeling better. A very young woman sitting on the bottom step nursing a baby answers softly, and the women around her slap their thighs and laugh. She has said something foolish, and now, seeing her mistake, she smiles too, shaking her head. Amina asks the question again, pointing to the picture in the book, looking from one face to another, and this time someone calls out a terse reply. Amina repeats the answer loudly: the baby is feeling better because her mother is giving her water. She turns the page again. Here is a jug of water and next to it—Amina explains, pointing—four lumps of sugar and a pinch of salt. If these are mixed with one-half liter of water, the baby will recover even more quickly because the salt and sugar help to replace the fluids lost to diarrhea.

We are facing an enormous *gawo* tree that rises solitary in the field of sand. Its great thorny branches are filled with nests spun from twigs and straggling wisps of straw: large, loose nests, tucked ragged into the crook of limbs. Baby egrets are taking little trial leaps and plunges, dropping from one branch and struggling up on new wings into another. Here and there, the sun shoots through the tree, flecking the deep orange of their legs and crests. There are storks as well, hunched beside their nests or sinking back into them; but the nestlings are hidden.

On a low branch, a male and a female stork are doing a dance. They face each other, lifting their wings high above their heads and slowly bringing them down. Their feet are moving rapidly in one spot, closing around the branch and letting go. But what made us look up in the first place is the rapid clack-clack-clack of their beaks, a sound like the long roll of castanets. To this unbroken rattle, their wings rise in a single motion, then come down in a slow sweep, closing over the soft underfeathers seen only in flight.

When Amina folds the book away, I follow her through the piece of cloth hanging in the doorway into the *dispensaire*. She is going to give the injections while Zara records in each child's *carnet* the name and date of the vaccine given. Today they are giving the BCG, which helps to protect against tuberculosis. They are also administering the immovax, a vaccine to counter polio, pertussis (whooping cough), diphtheria, and tetanus. It is given, Zara explains, to a child at scheduled intervals. The syringes have been laid out on a table that also holds an infant scale with a pink plastic basket. This room is smaller than its counterpart in Matameye, and because there is no electricity in Kantché there is no overhead fan. But again there is the poster of the two children, one emaciated, one fat and smiling, sitting on their mothers' laps. There is another poster of a woman holding a baby. She is surrounded by groups of food, each marked with the number of months at which it should be given to the infant as a supplement to breast milk: 3 *mois*—a bowl of *tuwo*; 6 *mois*—a round red tomato, one green bean, a fish, a cluster of groundnuts. There is also a standing scale against a wall and two chairs with iron legs and wooden seats. In an adjoining alcove, a number of large sacks are scattered on the cement floor with the words *Corn*

Soya Milk printed at the top of each. Below, a pair of clasped hands stands out blue between a band of stars and a band of stripes. Then, in large letters: *Furnished by the People of the United States of America. Not to Be Sold or Exchanged. Use No Hooks.*

Amina instructs the women to enter one by one. Each takes a turn rising from her spot on the steps and pushing back the cloth in the door, a child on her hip or beneath her *pagne.* Some of the children remember Amina in her white lab coat, and when they catch sight of her begin to cry and cling to their mothers. The mothers jiggle them up and down, trying to make them hush, while Zara looks up from where she is sitting with the *carnets* on her lap and smiles, making clucking noises, nodding her head. Then, while the mother holds the child still, Amina daubs its bare buttocks with alcohol and injects the vaccine. *"Shi ke nan,"* she says: it's all over. Afterward the screaming child refuses to be comforted, looks at its mother, aggrieved. The infants, too little to know why they are there, come in smiling, showing their new teeth. At the sting of the shot, they open their eyes in outrage before collapsing in tears.

As Amina herself must once have done, crying not for the loss of a whole, good leg but for the lightning arrival of pain, striking blind from a smiling sky.

Amina and Zara are at last putting everything away, packing up the syringes and vials, setting straight the pink plastic scale, when a woman pushes aside the cloth hanging in the doorway and asks if they will look at her baby. The flies buzz round her face in the midday glare.

Has she been here before, Zara asks. The woman clicks deep in her throat, lifting her chin in a gesture of assent, then enters and crooks her arm behind to hoist forward the bundle on her back. A child follows her in and stands by her side, a little girl of about eight, wearing a red head cloth. From her *pagne* the woman unwinds a long spindly creature, all bones. He is a year and a half, she says, but he lies along her arm, inert. His legs are little wandering sticks, unmuscled as a newborn's; his ribs stand out in sharp ridges. But his eyes are alert, comprehending, and when Amina bends forward he looks uncertainly at his mother for reassurance. Is this new person someone to be trusted? Is she all right?

But the mother seems a bit vacant, not quite there. What can be wrong? She has a dazed expression, as if she might be trying to remember what she has come for. It is the little girl who looks at the baby brightly, nodding encouragement. Zara asks the mother if she has any milk and she raises her blouse to show breasts that fall in empty plackets down her chest. The baby begins to whimper and she puts one of the breasts in his mouth, a pacifier. He sucks wearily, his eyes turned toward us, then lets go and begins to cry, a thin exhausted weeping. The little girl is following him anxiously, her forehead in furrows.

When Zara lifts him from his mother's arms and places him, sitting, in the baby scale, he leans forward to support himself on arms fragile as *gawo* thorns. Around his neck is a string with several amulets hanging from it, tiny stitched pockets of leather. Standing in front of the scale, Zara softly claps her hands, two, three times, nodding and smiling at him. He looks up, waiting to see what is next. Against the naked plates of his head, his ears coil flat and perfect. Zara turns her head to the side and looks at him out of the corners of her eyes. His jaw drops and the corners of his mouth twitch up, the beginning of a laugh. The mother seems scarcely to notice, but the little girl looks at us with the eager pride of a parent whose child has just distinguished himself before strangers. Have we seen how clever he is, how perfectly himself?

It is only much later that the mother's face returns, long after her *kwano* has been filled with pale yellow meal from a sack on the floor and she has disappeared with the baby and little girl across the sand into the bush. By then, it is the middle of the night and the air is stifling in Zara's little house. The face hangs in the burning darkness, the vague, insouciant eyes, the wavering smudge of the mouth. By then I know what Amina and Zara have read in the carnet, that this woman has had twelve children, that eight of them are alive, and that this child, at birth, was of normal weight. Now, eighteen months later, he weighs twelve pounds and it is probably—again the words that make the heart beat—too late. I have heard, too— Zara has told me it sometimes happens—a mother will stop taking care of a starving child. Will look absently in the other direction, refusing to answer questions. Hum tunelessly to herself. Forget to feed him water drop by drop.

Unwinding her baby from her *pagne,* she dropped her eyelids in a gesture I remember from some whirling place of half-forgotten dreams. Bridget McDonough—dim great-great-grandmother—scraping in the clay with a loy, the stench of rotting potatoes rising from the fields around her, infant tagged with medals of the Virgin tucked inside her shawl. The fluttering eyelids could be mistaken for indifference, even arrogance; but the gesture is one of shame. Flesh of my flesh, what have you come to? Close as my breath, as the clamor in my loins, your body appalls me. You are my own child.

Again and again, this dream. Lying on her back, a woman puts her hand on her stomach and realizes to her horror and astonishment that she is pregnant. In fact, she is more than a little pregnant. It is much too late. She simply had not noticed before. What in God's name is she to do? She can barely take care of the children she has. Her wits are scattered, another child will finish her off entirely. She is struggling to get to a window, frantic for a glimpse of trees blowing in the rain; but a child is climbing onto her lap, pulling her chin inward toward the room. She is terror-stricken. Five years before the child can go to school. And even then, years and years of facing in. She tries to think. Nursery school, naptime. But the terror builds and she wakes up shaking. She gradually realizes, with a wave of relief that breaks with supreme joy across her stunned body, that she is not pregnant at all.

Another dream. The woman has a baby boy but doesn't know what to do with him. He has red hair and blue eyes and the skin of an old, old man. The uncanny thing is that he looks at her with utter love, utter comprehension. In his ancient face his eyes are bright with forgiveness for a crime that has not yet been committed. And she loves him as she has never been able to love another human being. More than life itself. Then one day she looks at him and is horrified to see that he is almost dead with hunger. She has forgotten to feed him. She looks straight past his eyes, cannot bear to look into them. She is frantic with fear and guilt. What is she to do? She tries to think calmly, decides that if she feeds him conscientiously for even a week he will recover. That's what she'll do, she thinks, and then resolves the whole thing by going out to buy herself a new coat.

Here is something else, not a dream at all. It is the middle of the night and Zara, a few weeks old, is snuffling in her carry cot beside the bed. I silently beg her to wait, just until I have finished a dream on which my life depends. No, soon the snuffle has turned into shrill screams and I fold back the mosquito net, drag her onto my lap, and plop a breast in her mouth. She feeds on one side, then on the other. I stroke the top of her head, the dip of the fontanel, feel the plates of her skull one by one. I am trying to continue my dream sitting up, praying that she will soon have had enough and that we can both sink back into unconsciousness. Hastily, before she has time to look around, I tumble her back into the bed, cover her with the net, and in one motion fall back, stupefied, onto my pillow. But no, she is turning in the carry cot, I can hear her grunting, snuffling again. Go to sleep, I beg, for God's sake allow me to finish my dream. She is yelping now, little gasps and cries that finish in a long wail, the piercing scream of the newborn. I push the carry cot on its wheels back and forth, rocking her, trying to make her hush. But now she is screaming for life itself and beside myself, in a dark rage, I violently jiggle the carry cot until her screams are coming sharp and strangled.

Shaking with fear and deeply, deeply ashamed, I take her again from the carry cot and settle her on my lap, rocking her. Oh hush, hush, forgive, my daughter, forgive. When I fall back on my pillow, my eyes are wide open and I scarcely know what to think, much less to dream.

No, my mother, I will not forgive.

Tangled in the yellow sheets, a baby is sucking on an empty breast, its sweet milk gone. Gone, the hollyhocks along the hedge, the trees deep with summer. The mother strokes the baby's head, passes her hand over the bulge of its skull. Day and night, my tears are my food. Forgive me your hunger, forgive.

What is the day? The hour? The sun shines on a bed, stamps a thorny shadow on the sheets. In the window, berries bright as blood. A wheel flashing and turning, a prickly wreath of woe. Of all the trees that are in the wood, the holly bears the crown.

A child is standing on a ledge, in a door, holding onto her elbows. On the ceiling, a rainbow prism trembles and quakes. The short sweet stab of an icicle. The bed is empty, the mother is gone. Without so much as a wave, hello, goodbye, without a backward glance at the child awake in the night and cold, she is gone.

The mirror throws back a small face, drawn and freckled. Eyes like stones. No use looking for her, horrid child. You won't find her hiding in the closet or crouched in the bathroom. And she's not downstairs in the kitchen either, fixing you a nice cup of hot chocolate. Look all you want, you won't find her. She's gone and she's not coming back.

There was the night and there were the voices in it. The door opened and then closed. But in the time between, light falling onto the face turned sharply away. Not so much as a flutter of fingers goodbye. Take her away, bundle her out. Enough. Who needs her anyway, wretched thing. Out, get her out of here.

O, the rising of the sun!

For the love of Heaven, what is wrong with the woman? Too many children pressing at the door, that's what's wrong with her. No time to settle her wits, no time to sneeze or blow her nose.

Sing a song of chickadees, of starlings on a branch, scalding tears and speckled breasts, of icy breath on glass. When the stars threw down their spears, who looked up to see? Shadows leaping on the snow, catch me as I fall.

Go away, child, we've all had enough of you. Enough of your choked tears and temper, your sullen refusals to speak. Your mother, God have mercy on her, is lying at death's door in the hospital, your father is nearly distracted. And now you, old enough to be of some help with the younger ones, old enough to know better, what do we have from you but stamping feet and rages, temper from morning till night? You carry on like a wild creature. Can't you think of anyone beside yourself?

On the snow, the branches twitch giddy as lightning. The moon, and then the sun. Inside, the house is cold. The walls rise up silent as stone.

First there is winter, then spring. Spring is deadlier than winter, with its snowy fungus peeking through the blossoms on the silver tree. Bark like satin, glossy to the touch. And later on, cherries hanging in a cluster, some pecked to the pit. A boy high in the tree, and beneath it the child looking up, her hand on the trunk. The fungus mocks the white blossoms, flaunting its frill. But from below, you can see the sway of gills, the dark underwater ripple. Inside the house, someone sits in a chair with a white bandage wrapped around her head, trying to think.

In the thin gray light of dawn, the sound of foghorns. Then, as the day yawns open, an old woman stoops to pick mushrooms and drop them in a brown paper bag. Wrapped in her dark shawl, she doesn't know anyone is watching, but it is easy to see her from the window upstairs.

Here is the mother, here she is, home again and safe. She sits with a bandage round her head, her hands in her lap. Oh, look at her face, her poor thin face. How weary she is, arms limp as string. The child thinks she will die of grief. Where have you gone, my mother? And when will you return?

The mother is in the kitchen, stirring a pot. She is humming up and down to herself. The child is standing beside the stove, her arms around the baby straddling her hip. The baby is putting its fingers in the child's nose. The child takes the baby's wrist and pats her own cheek caressingly with the baby's flat hand. The mother bends down and takes the baby from the child, plants a long kiss on the baby's neck. "That's my big girl," the mother says, looking down at the child.

The child is sitting on the rocks, watching the mother move through the salty water beneath. The mother's legs are white and wavering, kicking apart and together. Her arms flutter out and back. The mother keeps her face carefully above water, but the wavelets are lapping at her chin.

Suppose the bones are not buried in the sand, waiting their moment. Suppose the bones are laid away in loamy earth, in dark clumps from which springs a summer garden. When you look all you see are delphinium, phlox, gypsophilia, shooting star. White butterflies are floating above lavender loosestrife. The air is scented and still. You lose yourself in the haze of summer. It is only in a dream that you see the body lying beneath, hands folded, eyes wide, but covered up, once and for all.

Shekaru ba su fa'di k'asa sai a jiki.
The years do not fall on the ground but on the body

Matameye, during the rainy season, is full of birds. Storks fly back and forth above the walls of the village, canny beaks pointing straight ahead. After a rain, they step to the edge of a pool, lower their necks, then throw back their heads. Or carry a few drops to the nest in the *gawo* tree where their babies wait with open beaks, straining blindly. The *gawo*, all thorns at this time of year, is also the home of the weavers. Their nests, round like hives, hang twenty, thirty, from the silvery limbs of a single tree. The weavers tip upside down at their nests, tiny feet clinging to the hole at the bottom, yellow breasts flashing. Anyone standing underneath can look up and see the storks lift out of the tree and, with a neat pliage of wings, sink back into it. From top to bottom, the branches are flecked gold with nervous underbellies.

Now and then the shadow of a stork glides across our path. Vast and ragged at wing spread, the dark figure on the sand sharpens at either end to a fleeting point. Zara and I are on our way to visit Hadiza, passing from beneath the odd tree out into a view of unbroken sky. It is late afternoon and the sun is still very hot. Hadiza lives in what Zara calls the suburbs of Matameye, a sloping field of sand on the far side of the paved road that runs north through Kantché and Takieta to

Zinder, south to Kano. This road marks the outer limit of the town. Beyond it, where Hadiza lives, the banco walls and shaded *zaures* are left behind in favor of straw huts, each occupying its own compound set apart from its neighbors by walls of plaited stalks. Whether it is the less traveled avenues of sand here that make walking seem like slogging across a beach, or the low bushes that take the place of neem and locust trees in the courtyards of Matameye, this place seems more starkly open to the sun. We keep our heads down, eyes averted from the glare.

The sand spilling over the thick rubber soles of our flip-flops burns our feet. We pass along the edge of the complex of huts, looking over walls onto goats and chickens and speckled guinea hens. There are children everywhere, jumping or standing still, hauling buckets of water. The huts are round, their roofs are cones of straw swirling to a point. In fact, wherever you look, there are round, scooped cavities: bowls holding grain or water, ladles and fat-bellied *tukunyas,* mortars blackening in the sun; calabashes filled with millet, *kwanos,* swollen gourds halved and hollow, iron cooking pots on their rings of stone. And encircling it all, the huts, the children, the dippers and kettles and cups, are the golden plaited walls, the outer ring.

The mud walls of Matameye do not keep their shape. Their contours are molded by wind and rain, are cracked open by the sun. When the rainy season is over they are repaired, just as these will be renewed with fresh millet stalks. But one mud wall always meets another to form an edge. They enclose by turning sharp corners. Here a wall is pliable at every point, bending to enfold and protect. It is made not of the earth but of what grows from it.

Hadiza is outside her hut, feeding her goats. She looks up at our approach and smiles. Since that first day at the Centre when she and Zara were weighing babies, when the mother of the boy swaying on the scale raised her fist, thumb up, I have seen Hadiza several times, both at the Centre and when she has come on night visits to Zara's and we've talked under the stars.

"So beautiful," Zara says, shaking her head when Hadiza is gone. "It's Hadiza who is the most beautiful woman in Matameye."

I have heard how Hadiza has been divorced for several years. Until recently she lived here in the hut with her daughter and with her mother, an invalid. Now her mother is dead; her daughter is eleven and lives with her father in Maradi, where there is a better school. Not long ago, Hadiza met someone from Kantché who pressed her to marry him, but she said she wouldn't be able to leave her work in Matameye. He said that was all right; on weekends he would come to see her here or sometimes she could go to Kantché. So it was agreed and now they are married but live apart, spending time together when they are able. Unlike the others at the Centre, Hadiza is paid a pittance. She has no training, but over time has gradually learned from the rest. At this point, she says, she is unhappy if she spends more than a few days away from her work.

She immediately invites us in, out of the sun. She herself has just come from the Centre, so we wait while she bends to the little corrugated tin door that has been fitted into the opening of the hut and turns the key in the lock. Then we all kick off our flip-flops at the entrance and take turns bending down to dip out of the sun into the darkened interior. A neighbor, an old woman with a goiter, has followed us inside, and when Hadiza and Zara and I sit down on a mat she squats a little behind Hadiza, watching. Light filters softly through the entrance, and in a minute the hut seems no longer dark inside but only comfortably screened from the sun.

Circles again, everything is in concentric circles, altogether different from Maimoun's rectangular inner court with its neem tree beneath the open sky. Rings of plaited straw, three in ascending order, bolster the conical thrust of the roof. At the center, the highest point toward which they spin, a handful of polished nuts hangs in a glistening cluster. The walls, too, are bound by rings. The straw between them tips one way, then the other, a zigzag, like lightning. Into one of the rings are stuck enlivening sprays of dried flowers and plants, into another a knife and a spoon. The floor is sand, spread with mats. Most of the space of the hut is taken up by a four-poster brass bed, high and narrow. It is covered by a pink sheet embroidered with delicate red flowers and green vines bright with swirling leaves. At the foot of the bed is an upturned box with a cloth over it to make a table; set out on top are little jars of cream and lotion, a bottle of eau de cologne with a spray on top, round boxes holding necklaces, bracelets, and earrings. And suspended from a rope tacked up against the curving wall are Hadiza's clothes: *pagnes*, blouses, scarves. Everything is neat, in place.

The sand beneath the mat where we are sitting is cool, and it is pleasant to sit here, ankles crossed, hugging our knees. Hadiza's kitten is glad to see her home at last. It sits on her lap and she strokes its back, scratching its neck where she has tied little leather pouches. She and Zara are talking about the food distribution last week, how they went out in the Land Rover to a place where crowds of women with *kwanos* had gathered to receive the corn, soy, and milk powder mixture that had been shipped in by CARE. All of them, Hadiza, Zara, the women, were in an uproar, yelling, pushing in the sun. Zara, caught up in the memory of it, claps her hands.

The old woman with the goiter crouching behind Hadiza seems to be listening to nothing. Her eyes are fixed on me. In her lower lip is a plug of tobacco, and every few minutes she turns her back on us, leaning outside the door of the hut to spit.

Hadiza's scarf is wound around her head and tied loosely at the top. It absurdly extends the line of her neck. In fact, everything about Hadiza is long: the arms twisted around the jutting knees, the feet placed side by side. Her arches, pressed together, make a hidden dome. She is quiet in her motions; only the involuntary catch in her breath belies the calm. The kitten has crawled off her lap and into the lap of the old woman, who ignores it. Hadiza tells us that the old woman, her neighbor—she gestures with her chin behind her—is a traditional healer and cares for people when the wind seizes them, asthma, and when they think they are losing their minds. That once when Marianma was staying with El Gouni, sometime after the death of her last baby, this old woman had visited and called on spirit after spirit in an effort to soothe her suffering. But Marianma was in a dream, she implored her baby to return to her, to drink from her breasts even then flowing with milk.

Hadiza and Zara continue to talk about work. This is the season for *malnouris,* they are saying, using the French word; now, in August, a couple of months before the harvest when the stores are depleted. Hadiza tells us about a child she helped to recuperate last year who gained weight bit by bit and is now healthy. The family brought the child in from the bush, she tells us, gasping a little, and now, at intervals, they come from their village to bring her gifts of food. Hadiza looks at each of us, then bends to call the kitten, who has disappeared underneath the bed. Behind Hadiza, behind the old woman who continues to stare at me, a chicken with a broken leg is walking around in the sun. It limps when it walks, one leg bent out at an angle, like a malplaced cane. When the kitten is safely restored to Hadiza's lap, Zara, watching Hadiza stroke its back, asks if she misses her daughter who has just gone to live in Maradi.

Hadiza lifts her elbows and sighs. If she hadn't gone away this time, she says, she'd have gone later. But she can't get used to her absence. Her daughter knew where everything was in the hut; if something were lost she could find it. For days after she left, Hadiza had kept waiting for her steps outside. At night she'd startle awake thinking she'd returned.

The old woman staring over Hadiza's shoulder is wearing a *pagne* tied just above her breasts, but the knot has come loose and one of her breasts has worked its way out. Her face is surrounded by wiry strands of gray hair that have escaped from the head scarf looped at the nape of her neck. Then, while Hadiza is staring off into space, lost in some vision of her own, the old woman speaks. She is looking straight at me. But with a crooked finger she points to Zara. Did I give birth to her? she asks.

I nod yes, I gave birth to her.

The woman continues to stare at my face, her eyes milky with age. To avoid the intensity of her gaze, I look down at the pinpoint of blood welling on my ankle. One of the prickly thorn bushes, surely, that Hadiza's goats were nibbling. The flies are droning black and sluggish. Trying to be discreet, I lick my finger and wipe the blood away, but it wells up again, and the flies return. Zara sends me an amused glance that says she sees what I'm doing. But also, perhaps, a glance to cover the uneasiness she may feel at this reminder that I gave birth to her, that here we are now, sitting side by side on the mat, but that at some moment in the past she slid out from the intimate spaces of my body. Then the old woman says something, mutters something with the plug of tobacco in her lip, that I don't understand. I look at Zara. "Dosso," she translates. "She says she saw you once before in Dosso."

It is my turn to stare. The word *Dosso* means nothing to me.

"Dosso. That's a town on the road to Niamey," Zara

explains, her voice neutral. Then, speaking in her ordinary, more animated, way, she says it doesn't sound likely. When would I ever have been in Dosso?

But for the moment I cannot attend to Zara's question. I am busy trying to think. The only time I was ever on the road to Niamey was seventeen years ago, during the year we lived in Zinder, when we traveled to the capital by bus. The road was still unpaved most of the way, and we had made the trip during the harmattan, when the wind was driving the sand forward in waves.

"She says that you had a baby," Zara translates. "You sat down with some women on a mat. They had babies, too." Zara looks at me with raised eyebrows. Her question has gone unanswered.

"It's possible we made a stop there the time we went to Niamey on the bus," I say briefly. "Not too long after your birthday. Do you remember?"

"I do," she replies, stopping short, and I think it must be the birthday she is remembering, not the bus. I am immediately sorry to have mentioned, in these circumstances, her sixth birthday, to have spoken casually, carelessly, of a moment which I know nothing about and which, for all I know, was still achingly present when she was making her first trip across Niger. Fear again strikes my heart, fear that she will tell me what transpired between us on that day, fear that she will not. But Zara seems unconcerned, has taken the kitten from Hadiza's lap and is scratching it behind the ears.

The old woman is watching me steadily. She appears in no hurry. "*Kusa ða Niamey,*" she says.

Not far from Niamey. Someplace before we got to Niamey and saw the River Niger shaded by willows; the water flowing in a steady stream beneath the trailing branches.

The old woman turns her back to lean outside the hut and spit. When she turns to face us again, her eyes, dazzled by the late sun, look around the hut uncertainly. She raises her head to stare up through the dusty shadows at the cluster of nuts. They hang motionless, caught in gravity's pull by the string. Even now, the polish on their skin of a few minutes ago has dimmed to accommodate the slipping light. She blinks at them slowly, three, four times, and when she looks down, her eyes come to rest again on mine. A light film covering the corneas blurs the distinction between the points of black and the surrounding brown. But within the oblique cast of her gaze, some dark patience holds its ground.

And then, as if the force of her memory is slowly nudging to life between us whatever she can see and I cannot, a shape begins to stir in the dust, a tree, a *gawo* tree, and underneath it a mat. A cool mat, just as now. There had been the sticks of sugarcane and then some women sitting on a mat in the shade.

With no change in her expression, holding my eyes with her own, the old woman leans forward and reaches out her hand to measure the distance from the ground of a child just old enough to stand.

I try to think. Dosso. It might have been Dosso, but then again it might not. One woman was braiding a little girl's hair and another was nursing a small child. Tulu was just standing on her new feet, and the woman nursing the baby had asked me how old she was. She had put the child she was nursing on her own new feet, and we had laughed when they looked at each other, then crawled back into our laps.

Is that it? Did it happen that way? Somewhere I asked a woman how many teeth her child had and then showed how Tulu still had only her front ones. But my memory has stopped short. Who she was, or where she was, in Dosso or elsewhere, is hidden. Surely she herself was too old, at that time, to have been one of the women sitting on the mats. She must have been the same age, more or less, that I am now.

The old woman drops her hand, but her eyes continue to

hold my own. I think with sudden irritation that I cannot follow her, that I cannot make this effort. How can I be sure if what I remember took place in Dosso, after all, given that Dosso was only a stop for gas and for prayers like all the others? What is to distinguish it?

And then, pulling myself up, recalled by her eyes to my task, I think, yes, the one thing I do not question is that we arrived in Niamey at sunset. So we may have stopped not too long before, not too far away, in Dosso, for the third prayer of the day, for *Asr*, chanted when the shadow of something is equal to itself, when the sun is still white hot in the sky but just about to slip into a zone of yellow. In Dosso it must have been like everywhere else, the men pouring water from their little kettles for ablutions, spreading their mats in the nearest stubbled field. "Oh Allah, cleanse me of my sins as a white garment is washed clean of sand."

Somewhere nearby there had been three women pounding in a single mortar. That I remember, at one of our stops, their pounding while Mike went off to buy sugarcane. In quick succession, each dropped her pestle with a thud, then threw it into the air over her head and clapped twice before catching it. In the distance, the backs of the kneeling men, bending, straightening. And close at hand, the quick beat of wood on wood, the hands clapping, the leaping pestles, the three bodies dancing for the evening meal.

The kitten is on its back, playing with a piece of thread that Hadiza is dangling above its nose, and Zara is looking at me. "I don't know where this happened," she says. "It may have been in Dosso or it may have been someplace else. But what I remember is that at one stop on that trip, while we were standing around waiting to get back on the bus, Lizzy and I tasted sugarcane for the first time. I remember, because I always think of that now when I see a child chewing on a stick."

And turning to the old woman, Zara tells her what she has told me. It is perhaps at the same instant that the vision rises before each of us. I have a sudden picture of Zara and Lizzy standing beside the mat, wherever it was, sucking on their sugarcane, hair blown straight out from their heads, stiff with dust. And just as I am thinking what strange creatures they must have looked, white faces streaked with red dust, hair electrified, the old woman raises her hands to her head and unmistakably sweeps them straight out in either direction.

Then, for the first time, the old woman drops her gaze. She examines her feet. She unloops her *pagne* and knots it higher, covering both breasts. When she speaks she looks at Zara and says something so rapidly I can make out nothing except "*yata*," my daughter. Once, as she speaks, she hits her breast with her fist.

Nor does Zara translate immediately. Instead, her face assumes a look of commiseration and she inclines her head, pronouncing the expression used in times of sorrow. *Assha, Assha,* she croons. Her hands are pressed together in front of her, as if in prayer, and she slices them up and down a little, for emphasis. Oh, *Assha.*

The old woman, who has been looking at Zara, now turns to gaze again at me. Zara turns as well, then, and tells me—and she says she's not sure if she's understood, not sure if she's got the story straight—that one of the women on the mat, a woman with a little walking child, had been this old woman's daughter. The old woman says she had been sitting on the mat with her; that's how it happened she saw me and remembered.

But, Zara says, whether she has understood all this correctly or not, she's sure of the rest. The daughter died in childbirth sometime soon afterward. The old woman was on her way to visit her, to be with her when her second child was born, but she arrived too late. Now she sometimes dreams that she is on her way to find her daughter and that she has not died at all, that the baby is still to be born, that everything is as it was, that she is sitting with her on a mat—and here Zara hits her own breast with her fist exactly as the old woman had done—just as she had been sitting on that day long ago in Dosso when we had joined them. That she is sitting with her daughter as Zara and I are sitting together even now in Hadiza's hut.

It is again my turn to stare. The old woman stares back, milky eyes alight. For a long moment we hold each other's gaze. Then, just as I am about to drop my eyes, she extends both her hands, thumbs up, and gripping one of Zara's hands in one of her own, and one of mine in the other, raises our clasped hands, shaking them a little, lifting them together in the air as high as she can reach, straining upward, up toward the cluster of nuts that in the slipping light have now taken on a dark and glossy sheen.

When it is time to leave, we bend down one after another and file out of the hut. We say goodbye to the old woman, but Hadiza is going to walk with us a little way along the path back into Matameye. When the goats see that she is about to leave they strike up a frantic bleating, and she has to turn and tell them she won't be long. Her reassurances seem not to soothe them at all because we can hear them still as we walk past the rush walls and swirling roofs. When we look back, finally, to call out to them again, the old woman is still standing where we left her. Her hands are in the air, palms tapping on either side of her face, cradling in a gesture of farewell all we have left unsaid.

Mai iɗo ɗaya ba ya goɗe Allah sai ya ga makaho.
The one-eyed man does not thank Allah until he sees a blind man.

In back of the Centre Medical, in the large sandy court where several neems splash their shade, loose clusters of women have gathered in two corners. At the center of each group a lively fire leaps blue and yellow against the sides of a large black pot. *Kunu,* a kind of porridge, is being prepared. Collected around one fire are the mothers of the severely malnourished children who remain for supervised care in a bungalow at the far end of the court. A woman with a baby on her back is standing over the pot stirring millet. Today it is her turn to show the others, and it is their turn to observe. First she roasts the raw grain at the bottom of the pot because millet broken down in this way is easier on the deteriorating intestines of the children. Then she pours water into the pot and stirs the mixture. In the opposite corner Hadiza, her scarf wound to a stiff point above her head, is demonstrating to a group of women how to prepare *kunu* for a healthy child of six months who will not be weaned for another year. She stirs ground millet and water together, then adds *kuli-kuli,* a peanut extract that includes protein. As the long handle of the spoon makes a slow circle around the edge of the pot, Hadiza's elbows point out, then in.

Further along on the back step of the Centre Medical where I am sitting, the afternoon after Zara's and my visit to Hadiza's hut, Maimoun is nursing Fasuma. Now that Fasuma is five months old, Maimoun has brought her for her second immovax. Zara and Maimoun had together winced, a little while ago, just before Zara had firmly rubbed alcohol where the needle would plunge. I would like to ask Maimoun more about Talatuwa—about the dream of Talatuwa as the little baby she sheds bitter tears to see lying there without a cloth or dress, naked, without a bracelet for her ankle or wrist, a baby she snatches up only to find transformed into a girl with budding breasts—but my Hausa is not up to it, and here is one circumstance in which I cannot ask Zara to act as interpreter. Instead, falteringly, I try to tell Maimoun about our encounter with the old woman in Hadiza's hut, how strange it was she should have recognized me after so many years. Maimoun is holding Fasuma's feet in one hand, playing with her toes, and as she listens she meditatively nods her head to show me she has understood. "You are not a stranger here," she says slowly, and although with every day Niger seems more and more a place that Zara and I inhabit together, I am jolted by Maimoun's statement. However lost in the shadows I might have been seventeen years ago, the world around me had eyes to see.

When I begin to tell the story of the old woman's daughter, how she died soon after in childbirth, Maimoun turns full face to look at me. Her eyes are large with fear: fear, I think, because I have clumsily related to a woman who is likely to have more children a death by childbirth. Zara has told me that she has seen more than one woman die giving birth at the Centre, and that each time it makes her a little more frightened to have a child someday herself.

But the fear in Maimoun's eyes soon gives way to pity, and we exchange a long look. Here we are, at least for this moment, sitting in the blazing sun: Fasuma lying safe in her lap, Zara, also safe so far as I know, working nearby in the bungalow.

We are company, sitting together on the step, a little out of things. What we cannot see, what I have never seen, is the little morgue behind where bodies wrapped in white sheets—adults, for the most part; a child can easily be wound in a *pagne* and carried away—wait to be removed for burial. We are looking, rather, into the court visible in front of us; under the feathery branches of neems, women's *pagnes* and head-scarves make dappled spots of color: dark green, vermilion, mustard yellow. The late afternoon light is deepening. Among the hens and guinea fowl, a peacock is stepping on the sha-dow-splotched sand, his tail trailing long and light. His neck is silvery blue, flashing beneath the crowned head.

A half-hour ago, when I had stood with Zara in the bun-galow reserved for the gravely ill, we had seen him through the doorway. On one of the beds a little girl sat in a white shirt, a string of amulets around her waist. Her eyelids drooped, her arms and legs were threaded bone. Zara took the dipper and scooped some water from a *tukunya* and showed the woman sitting beside her how to help her to drink, drop by drop. This child is getting well, Zara had said; if you had seen her last month. To me it looked as if she had scarcely strength to draw breath. On another bed, a child lay completely hidden by a *pagne*, protection, perhaps, from the flies. But here and there the *pagne* twitched, grew quiet. Across the third bed a child lay unable to lift his head. He lay still, breathing shallowly, his mouth cracked and torn. When Zara had leaned over him with the dipper, he had turned his head away, had whimpered and closed his eyes.

In a patch of sunlight beyond the doorway, a lizard rushed in the path of the strutting peacock. At once the peacock had stepped back and, shivering all over, had raised its tail. Through the frame of the door we had seen the many eyes glimmering in their moon sockets.

Was this the doorway where he had stood, the man with the lime? The man standing at death's door? He had been staying with his little daughter at the hospital; she was severely malnourished, and it was clear to everyone she couldn't last more than a day or two. He had begged to be told what he could do to help. Wasn't there something that would make a difference? He implored anyone who would listen: tell me; whatever it is, I'll get it. One night, late, more to get rid of him than anything else, someone had said a lime, maybe if the child could eat a lime. Immediately he had run out into the street, stopping the few people who were passing. But nobody was carrying a lime, and because it was the middle of the night the vendors were gone. He rushed from compound to compound, waking people, calling out for someone to give him what he needed. *Sabo da Allah,* for the love of God, a lime. At last an old woman had shuffled out, extending the small green globe on a flat palm. He had snatched it and raced back through the dark streets.

During the time he was gone the child had died. But the point was that nobody could make him understand it was too late. He had stood there in the doorway with the lime in his hand, completely at a loss. He'd found the lime; surely, surely now his child would live.

Yau gare ka gobe ga wani.
Today is yours, tomorrow belongs to another.

Zara is out dancing. One of the *fonctionnaires* she knows in town is being moved to another part of the country and a group of his friends is seeing him off. Of course I'll be all right, I tell her, so glad you're going, it will be nice here by myself tonight. She kicks off on her mobylette and I close the iron gate behind her. Because the wind is rising, I go inside instead of sitting outside in front of the house. A lightbulb hangs from the ceiling shaded by an inverted calabash, and I draw up a chair beneath it. I am reading the poems of Anna Akhmatova in a collection I gave Zara on her nineteenth birthday, a book she has brought with her and keeps in the scaffolding of the Hausa bed tipped up against the wall to make a bookcase. Perhaps I read because I don't want to look around too much, don't want to picture Zara on all the nights she has been here alone, content or lonely. It's a kind of reticence, perhaps of the sort she, too, experiences in connection to me. To allow myself to imagine too boldly her most solitary, personal moments, or moments of intimacy with others, seems a violation of the closeness of our bond. There are questions I do not ask.

On the day of my arrival, after Zara had made the bed with my mother's yellow sheets, after we were sitting inside with the fan flying above our heads, a glass of Pepsi in hand, she said she'd show me what she did when she got lonely or depressed. She pressed a button on her tape recorder and the room was filled with the sounds of Jimmy Cliff. Zara was immediately on her feet, head turned slightly to one side, hips moving lightly, delicately, to the strong reggae beat. The harder they come, they harder they fall, one and all. I joined her in singing the last word, sliding up, then down. At home we danced to this music together, thumping and shouting.

Zara has told me that in Matameye you do not dance in front of your mother, and I am aware that however freely Zara danced to Jimmy Cliff on the day of my arrival she will dance very differently with her friends tonight. In Maimoun's dream, her daughter Talatuwa had turned her back and walked straight out into the noonday sun. And I cannot forget how in order to escape the maternal gaze, this is where I myself once came, here to Africa.

Koumia: shame. It may, too, have something to do with the elders, some sharp compound of triumph and despair. Yes, I will take your place. With a child of my own, I will be the one to decide. You, on the other hand, have only the impotence and debilities of age to look forward to. Despite all your care to keep me from eating the seeds of the pomegranate, to keep me your own child forever, I have roamed and enjoyed. Turning my back on you, I have experienced delight.

I am at home, now, in the dark. It is here I have learned to know my image in the mirror, here, where you are not. When he first touched my hair, I wanted to cry out that it belonged to another. I was seized with shuddering. I had expected his hands to be clumsy, but they instructed me in a delight I knew I could have died for. When the dark wave washed over me, I closed my eyes for the first time to the passionate limpidity of your gaze and felt a seed—so deeply planted I had no name for it—root and stir.

That was the secret you tried to keep from me with all your anxieties and precautions: the sweetness of the flesh. And why? Because you knew that the fulfillment of desire spells the end of your day and the beginning of mine. There is no going back: the new generation is already looking for a hidden place in which to unfurl.

But despair as well. Oh my mother, how can I endure the signs of your collapse! To leave my place at your side, the cool shade of your protection. And in this challenge to your authority, this push of the door in your face, do I place myself beyond the pale of your love? Do I invite some blow from which I shall never recover?

And so I pretend not to know what is happening, to deny the child of my flesh who is also of yours. When you ask me her name, I know to turn my face away in shame. When you remove her from my breasts, to care for and keep, I dare not refuse.

It was all delight down on the coast of Nigeria, at Igbobi, so far away from the elders. In the morning, before dawn, Mike and I lay in bed upstairs and heard the roosters answering each other under the window. Without waking, we stretched length to length. In the afternoons we made love when the heat was most intense, then filled the tub with cold water and sat in it looking into each other's faces over the tops of our knees. I took in the clean fold of his eyelids, the black eyes oblique in the watery light. The bathroom had been a room like any other before it had been fitted out with a sink and toilet and tub raised on claw feet, a tub long enough for a tall man to stretch full length. The slatted shutters were closed over the window and the sunlight fell in bars on the mahogany planks of the floor.

From below we could hear the voice of a schoolboy who was up from his siesta and looking for the principal. Soon the boys would be out on the field playing cricket, and Mike would be with them. I might go out and watch, or I might sit in a canvas chair on our upper porch and watch the quick slide of the sun toward the horizon. At the equator it sets all at once, and then the cicadas, throbbing whenever you stop to listen throughout the long hours of white heat, become deafening.

But the stairs of the house, the outdoor wooden steps that were the only means of reaching the rooms above where the long afternoons awaited us. They mounted away from the house to a landing, a little lookout of its own, where they made a sharp turn and folded back to the house and to the porch above. The staircase was overhung with a sheet of corrugated tin so that our climb was either shaded from the blistering sun or safe from a downpour. The bannisters and rungs were painted a light gray like the steps themselves and woven with vines whose wide leaves spread cool and green. During the rainy season the vines shot tendrils that groped blindly in the air, upward, out, like an inchworm careening on a leaf. The stairs, then, top and bottom, became a bower of delicate blossom, fluted, fragrant, blue like morning glory.

Up the stairs and down, Ben Waleru: that one. His back beaded with sweat as he rubbed our mahogany floors with the sawed-off end of a coconut shell. Mansion wax, that's what he preferred. Java water, to bleach our clothes. He opened the shutters in the dining room before we came down for breakfast, put a bowl of yellow allamandas in the center of the table. A grilled tomato, a fried egg, always a plate of toast turned in drippings, a pot of tea. He had worked as a cook on the Elder Dempster line, making stops along the coast at Accra, Monrovia, Freetown, Las Palmas, before the long stretch up to London. Ben had four children, three daughters and a son, Douglas, a little boy with a bad cough. Now his wife was going to have another baby, maybe in January, maybe in February. All this he told us after he had served dinner to us beneath the fan, while we sat in our chairs, turning our empty glasses, and he stood on one bare foot with the other resting on it. Did we like snails? Because if we did he would find some in the garden and cook them for us. And trifle, he could do that too, and steak and kidney pie. The fan slowly cut the air while below moths with dark wings circled our heads, flitting from one of us to another.

Twenty-three years old, we sat appalled and content with our lot, a man of forty-five at our complete service.

Every morning at seven-thirty, the vice principal flung a bell up and down, and we gathered, boys and teachers, in front of the chapel that stood a little apart. The sun was lifting whole and heavy above the rim of the cricket field. An hour later the sweat would be standing on our foreheads. Assembled, we filed inside, the smallest boys first, eleven or twelve years old, knees still round and childish beneath the pleats of their starched khaki shorts. They had only recently come to school from towns and villages as far east as Calabar, from Onitsha where the ferry ran back and forth across the Niger, from Benin in the midwest, from Abeokuta and Ilorin, and from Lagos itself. But very few from the dry savannas of the north, from Kano or even Kaduna, where Mohammed was honored. Igbobi College had been founded jointly by the Church of England and the Methodists, and once inside the chapel, the air moving lightly through the windows, we sang the doxology.

Crotons, flame trees with leaves too green, flowers too red, poinsettia, jasmine soaking the air. Bananas in an afternoon swelling to unspotted yellow. Orchids trampled in the mud. Avocado trees dropping their fruit in our path. In the markets, where women sometimes reached out a flat hand to place against my swelling stomach, the tables were stacked with squash, tomatoes, and eggplant. Yam chopped into pieces. Cassava, plantain, corn, manioc, and beans. Lemons as big as a child's head, persimmons, figs, guavas, green oranges, limes, coconuts. Palm wine. Groundnuts and eggs. Prawn from the bay, fish sold in buckets. After a rain, the sun drew steam from the earth. In the forests on the road to Ibadan, vines twisted from tree to tree, mahogany, rubber, palm. On the ground by the side of the road, they wound in and out of the skeletons of cars and lorries that had come to grief, covering them until there was only a leafy mound.

Two years, that was the time we would have, moving back and forth every day between the upstairs and down, passing along the path to the schoolrooms. One night, a month or so after we arrived, while fastening the shutters of the dining room after dinner, I imagined I was throwing the bolt for the last time, that the house was being closed up once and for all. No more sitting at noon with the fan turning overhead and looking through the windows cut deep in chalk-white walls at hibiscus bright red on the other side, stamens drooping in the heat, at the glitter of sun birds above them, the scattering of yellow pollen. No more plates of sliced avocado surrounded by wedges of lime, no more prawn that came from the bay. No more pausing halfway up the steps at night to look at the shining coil of glowworms in the grass below. No more classrooms of boys sitting row after row, curious, wry. No more Kpaduwa, Ogedegbe, Ajayi. No more afternoons with the light falling through the slatted shutters onto the mahogany floors. No more waking in the night to the overwhelming throb of cicadas, no more radiant mornings dripping with last night's rain. It was all over before it had fairly begun, all bathed for the first time in the transforming light of desire.

But what I could never understand, sitting in the bathtub, was the way his neck rose in a steady column above the neat simplicity of his collarbone. It was the neck of a boy, rounded still, and smelling of pine. The miracle was that it could be sturdy and slender at the same time, a shapely trunk perfectly designed to hold aloft a jaw, a chin dipped in honey. The mouth stayed in place, long and full, but the slope beneath the lower lip slid into a crevice, a dark place folded in on itself, a recess I could reach out and touch. Above all this the wide gaze, a distance that dissolved and slipped, a snowslide.

We spent whole afternoons in the bathtub, its sleek white sides a guarantee. A place of counsel and forgetting. The womb of the world, we called it.

Zara entered the language of our love before we knew anything about her. He rested his head on my stomach, whispering endearments. "Tiny Oridota," he said. "Come out and play with us."

When the rains begin, Zara is still out dancing, and I am reading the first lines of one of the poems in the book: "Suddenly it was quiet everywhere, the last of the poppies had blown away." The ping ping of single drops on the iron roof is almost immediately followed by a steady rumble, and then the sting of rising dust. There is a crack of thunder, and a second later the light goes out. The room is plunged in darkness so profound I have to tell myself where I am. This is Matameye and I am sitting with a book on my lap. Zara and I together heard the fourth call to prayer, *Maghrib*, when we were sitting down at her table eating rice and sauce, just after the sun had newly slipped out of sight beyond the horizon. But now the sky is completely black and we have entered the zone of night.

I am alone in this house. Despite the lightning, despite the thunder that splinters the sky, there is no chance of a child waking in fear or of my having to grope through the pitch dark to give comfort. No chance of sitting next to the child and droning in a singsong voice, listen to the rain, how it is falling on the fields around us, how the tender shoots are stretching for happiness, how the roots are reviving at the scent of water, drinking deeply at last, how in the morning the air will be cool and the new leaves will glisten in the sun. I, like El Gouni on the other side of the wall, El Gouni who is praying always for the peace that Allah gives, who is awaiting Marianma's arrival this night or another, am watching over no uneasy sleep. All over Matameye people are listening with grateful hearts to the rain, women with babies lying across their laps, babies nursing in their arms, women with breasts uncovered to tiny mouths. There is the rooting and snuffling, the brief cries that open to a wail. Then the drugged tunneling from sleep, the tiny arms frantically clutching the air, the helpless mouth clamped to the breast, the sturdy gulps, the soft elbows tucked behind as they sit drinking, drinking for all they are worth.

For a bare instant the light flickers on and then off, but not before I have had time to take in the hand resting on top of the book. It is not the hand of a young woman. It startles me, the sight of my hand detached from all the rest. Yesterday evening Zara and I were on our way to Maimoun's when we passed two children selling groundnuts. One child was lying on a bench, a kerosene lamp at her head. The other was sitting on the sand below, cross-legged beside the nuts set out there: little tins of six or seven, arranged precisely in concentric circles. It made a picture, the ring of golden light on the sand, the shadow of neem branches above their heads; and far above, the startling presence of the stars.

Then, out of nowhere, someone threw out a greeting: *Sannu Tsohuwa.*

A word Zara has taught me; *Tsohuwa:* a crone, an ancient. But where was she? Who did they mean? I could think of Deje, breasts hanging down her chest in flaps; and another woman who lives in a hut on the road to the Centre and whom we call "the oldest woman in the world." She is a figure from a fairy tale, bent double at the waist, groping her way with a stick. Her skin is mottled white on black, as if time has forgotten who she was. Old. Then, in an appalled moment, I understood.

"Oh, they mean it respectfully," Zara said, turning her face to me. "They say it to be polite."

How could I explain that courtesy only made it worse? A slighting remark might be farfetched, a lie; a compliment intends, at least, to pay tribute to the truth. In Matameye I am addressed publicly as what I am: a woman whose children are grown. And I remember the story Zara told me of the old woman who had come to the Centre asking for the medicine that would allow her to have another child; she had heard they measured women's stomachs at the Centre to see how many children were still inside them. Someone told her yes, they did measure the growth of a baby inside the mother, but had no medicine to make an old woman pregnant. She had shaken her head and gone sadly away.

No, certainly it's not to have a child again. It's rather that the question continues to perplex: where did they go, the ones that were there? A child is conceived, there is nothing to tell you such a thing has happened: later, when you do know, nothing to convince you. But with the first edgy flutterings, felt so close to the region of the heart, comes the startled realization that someone else is there; and with it, the dim reminder that "else" means "other." Before you have even seen the face of this coiled presence, have been left gasping and astonished that there should be any pain in the world so tearing as this of the first separation, the movement away has begun; the bone to harden, the limbs to stir. And then, without even noticing how it happens, the habit of loving this small creature becomes ingrained, becomes more and more difficult to break. But break the habit of loving? Who would ever want to? No, it's rather that the habit has taken on, without one's being aware of it, all the characteristics of passion: the intense preoccupation, the fear of loss, the terrible regrets for the misshapen forms love has taken, for the injuries inflicted, both known and unknown, and then the sudden, unaccountable joys.

One afternoon, not so many years ago, we were walking, my mother and I, beneath winter branches. We passed a hospital and, above its door, the great face of a clock. The black hands were pointing in the sun. The short one was fixed at the Roman numeral three, the longer one only a minute or two beyond. Together they cast a deep shadow on the white face of the clock. Above us, the row of silver trees waved their branches in the wind. I tried to put my hand in my mother's, slip the back of my hand inside the palm of hers. What I felt was the shape of one empty hand cradling the emptiness of another. Seventeen minutes after three, told twice.

Gone. The earth yawns open and the beloved daughter is no longer there. Gone, simply. Is she lost to sleep, to nuptials celebrated in the darkness of the underworld, to death? She was wandering in a field of asphodel, her hair floating in the quiet lap of summer. What has her mother to fear, in the haze and drone of a flawless day? She thinks of her daughter stooping to break a lily far down at the base of its stem, of the pungent release of its perfume. She thinks of her feet stepping between the long blades of grass. Then, out of nowhere, she hears screams of a kind to make her blood run cold. At first a fit of trembling overtakes her so violent she cannot move. In the perfect terror of the instant, she knows that this is what she has waited for, night and day. Then, her heart thrashing in her breast, she lunges forward to meet the rush of the future. But where she had expected, dreaded, to find an injured or despairing child, there is nothing. A field of asphodel, stupid beneath the sun. All she can think of is her daughter's floating hair, the way it lifts from the back of her neck in the wind. Completely beside herself, she rushes back and forth, afraid she is losing her mind. Perhaps she was mistaken in the spot, perhaps her child, already too weak to moan, lies bleeding in the grass. But desperately as she searches, asking of the sky, the blank earth at her feet, what became of the daughter whose hair she tended with ribbons and combs, there comes back to her only the long wink of silence. The meaningless flash of a bird's wing, pollen enough to make her swoon. In the spin of the afternoon, in the giddy rush of the season, she stamps her foot on the ground, once, twice, in a fury that drives down, always down. Then nothing! There will be a plenitude of nothing! Not a seed will break, not a root will stir. The loamy earth will be wrapped in wind, in devastation. The rising sun will be greeted with infertility. And in every mouth the taste of hunger. In every stomach the empty beat of a drum. Let it be general, the rich harvest of grief!

But later on, when her daughter is at last again at her side, when the fields are restored and the ears of corn plumping their sheaves, it is already too late. Her own child's lips are stained with red.

Arziki rigar k'aya.
Wealth is a coat of thorns.

A few days later, Amina is braiding Zara's hair. We sit on the steps of the *dispensaire* in Kantché, Amina one step above Zara, opposite the *gawo* tree. The work for the morning is over and Zara is leaning against Amina's knees, dozing. Amina sections off tiny portions of Zara's scalp and makes a braid of each, about six of them, then winds another braid around the lot. Bunched together they make a little jet that springs from Zara's head. Then Amina takes her scarf and ties it with a large knot on one side of Zara's head. She considers the effect, unloops it, and ties it on the other. Last, she arranges it on top.

While this is going on, Haïz, a young man in a white lab coat, a first-year medical student who has just begun to work in Kantché as part of his training, comes and sits with them on the steps. In a desultory fashion Amina and Zara have been talking about marriage. They are saying that they will introduce to each other all the men they know and together pick the best of the lot. Then they will be cowives. Haïz says no, no, it's impossible; women living in the same household never get along together. When he was a few years old, he says, hands deep in the pockets of his coat, his mother had died giving birth to his younger sister and a cowife had brought him up. His father had two wives and it hadn't worked out. "It's impossible to share everything exactly," he says, the scar twitching in his eyebrow.

Amina is looking critically at Zara's hair, which is coming loose from its braids. She flicks her fingers at the little unraveling jet, dismissing it. Haïz says that he is the first one in his family to go to school, that he grew up in a village way out in the bush, not far from here. At first nobody wanted him to go to Niamey; it was too far away, too different. Now his family is proud of him, he says, speaking to Amina and to Zara, whose eyes have opened. He goes back to the village whenever he can, but they have no idea what his life is like. Their ideas are not his. For example, marriage. He knows for himself that he'll never take more than one wife.

Amina shakes her head and makes a sucking noise with her teeth. "That's what they all say when they're young," she says. "Just wait twenty years."

But she is already on her feet. She and Zara and I are going to visit the palace of the *sarki* of Kantché, the Chef de Canton, to thank him and his wives for the gift of an omelette and sauce they sent to Amina and Zara at work last week, and to thank him silently, I think, for the dispensation he gave Maimoun's sister, Koubra, so that she might leave her husband of one night and marry the man she preferred.

For a moment we all stand on the steps looking at the immense *gawo* tree, at the baby egrets plunging off one branch and fluttering up into another, their bright orange legs and crests flickering in the silver branches. Several *kwanos* have been tucked in between the roots of the tree. I had noticed them earlier and thought they must have been left there by women coming to the *dispensaire*, to be retrieved later on when they left. But the women are gone and the *kwanos* are still there. Amina explains it's because this ancient *gawo* is thought to have special powers, that people come from far away to leave offerings. Haïz stands on the steps in his lab coat, reflecting, shaking his head.

Then he wishes us goodbye: he'll see us all later, tomorrow, someday soon.

It is one o'clock in the afternoon and the sun is hot. We are not going far, the high walls of the palace are visible from the clinic, but we walk slowly, taking our time. Amina sinks sideways on her left leg, heel wobbling uncertainly before subsiding delicately in its flip-flop. She and Zara are holding hands, and she leans a little into Zara with every other step. I am trailing behind, watching them together, teasing, laughing, and feeling left out. What am I doing here in the first place, a *tsohuwa*, like El Gouni the mother of a grown child, wandering through a wasteland of sand in the full blaze of the sun?

The face of the *sarki*'s palace in Kantché is broken by the lines of the raised *zaure*, lines that subtly incline toward each other as they rise. At the top, each gives way to a blunted minaret, curved on one side like a crescent. A high window, blank and dusty, looks out from an elaborate design standing in relief: long smooth rectangles cross to make an *x*; at the center, a shape like a diamond. Below, a guard stands within the slender shade of the massive doorway. He is in green and red motley, like the *ɗogarai*, the guards outside the palace in Damagaram. And as in Damagaram—ancestral Hausa name for the region of Zinder—swallows flutter in and out beneath the heavy beams of the doorway into the sunlight.

◆   ◆   ◆

A doorway like the one from which he had set out, the *sarki* of Damagaram, seventeen years ago, at Ramadan. There had been all the weeks of fasting before: Zinder—during the hottest months of the year—had neither eaten nor drunk while the sun was in the sky. Weeks during which a crier had walked through the streets before dawn alerting the sleeping population to rise and fill their bowls before the sky grew light.

And then one evening a child in the street had pointed to the new moon in the west, barely visible in the haze of the setting sun. Late into the night the city had been alive with the sounds of clapping and singing, of drumming and the flare of fireworks.

Before dawn we had walked to the prayer ground. The sun had barely sprung free of the horizon when, with one motion, everyone stepped back, clearing a path. Seven or eight barefoot boys galloped headlong up the center of the crowd, their horses hung with saddle cloths glinting silver and gold. One by one they abruptly pulled in the reins, sending the animals' heads up with a jerk, then fell back into a gallop. Behind them trotted a stately line of horses bearing men with enormous drums fastened at their sides. They beat the drums with long sticks, hooked at the end, keeping up a steady tattoo, an intimate ba-boom, ba-boom that drew the crowd together, breathless. Then, breaking in from far away, wailing and whining, rose a high metallic note, an unearthly sound, pleading with the drumbeat. A man on a shining black horse trotted forward, his slender horn, eight feet long, held to the sky: the *kakaki*, a horn like the ones in Uccello's *Battle of San Romano*, burnished metal catching the sun. Finally, under a canopy held above his head by a horseman trotting just behind, rode the *sarki* of Damagaram himself, turbaned, swathed in white robes. He sat upright, the gold tassels of the canopy swaying around his face. His courtiers trotted on each side of him, ceremonial in red and green motley, leather sheaves of arrows slung over their shoulders.

And last of all, in the dust raised by the others, bringing the procession to a close, danced the court jesters, leaping, whirling, making faces at the crowd.

Soon afterward, in a silence that swelled like a long indrawn breath, everyone removed their shoes. They spread their mats in front of them, and stood with hands at their sides facing east toward the *Ka'bah*. The imam intoned a prayer and, in one swift motion, hands were raised to shoulders, right over left, and lowered again. Palms were lifted, turned over, and dropped. A thousand people bending from the waist, kneeling at the same instant, lowering their foreheads to the sand. "O Allah, set me apart from my sins as the east is set apart from the west. Glory to you, our Lord, and all praise. O Allah, forgive me."

Amina greets the guard and asks for the *sarki*. He is not here today, the guard says, but after Amina and Zara confer for a moment they decide we'll go in anyway to pay a visit to the *sarki*'s wives. As we pass from beneath the full gaze of the sun into the interior of the *zaure*, cool descends on us like a blessing. But it takes a moment for our eyes to adjust to the sudden shade. There are two massive columns, white, with dark painted designs running down them. And stuck in the wall above the entrance, sheltered by the beams that gird the ceiling of the *zaure*, is some odd structure that looks like a collection of shards, perhaps the rounded fragments of a broken *tukunya*. Then we glimpse the swallows peeking in and out and see that these are nests, built from mud and particles of woven mat.

Beneath the arch that opens into the airy spaces of the adjacent chamber, the swallows swoop back and forth, twittering. We follow them through the passage and then through another and another. There is vaulting everywhere, cool deep spaces that make us forget the sun. Heavy columns rise at intervals from the smooth floor and from them springs a play of arches, some ogival, others round. They soar above our heads, pivot in place. In one corner, a flight of steps ascends against a wall, leading to spaces we can't see: a balcony, perhaps, or sleeping chamber. Along the edges of the columns, across the floors, the shadows are deep and still. But a candle carried up the steps at night must make the vaulting spin. The swallows dip from one chamber to another, beneath the arches, above our heads. Once Amina twists her neck and looks at Zara and me with her smile of a wise gnome. "Don't we wish," she asks, "that we too had wings and could fly away whenever we liked?"

At last we stop and look back. From where we stand, we see a procession of three arches, each diminishing in the embrace of the one behind it. At our feet, a large coin of sunlight quivers on the floor. We look up between two columns to a lofty round window, a radiant eye.

We have been walking through the reception rooms. Now we pass from the last one into a large open court, the *cikin giɗa*, startlingly bright after the walls we have left behind. The sunlight dazzles. Several neems make splashes of shade on the sand and in the middle, equidistant from each of the rooms opening onto the court, is a large thatched roof raised on poles. Underneath, on mats spread liberally on the low platform that makes a floor, a number of women are sitting with their children around them. When we walk into the court, the women nearest to us look up and call out a greeting. They know Amina and Zara already, and when they are told I am Zara's mother, they nod and look smilingly from one of us to the other. One old woman taps open hands in the air, her head to one side. We too sit down on the mats, out of the sun, and one by one, sometimes at intervals of a minute or two, each of the many women greets us, attentively inquiring about our work, our family, the afternoon we inhabit together. Zara has told me that these women are not all wives, that some are sisters of the *sarki*, his grown daughters, his aunts and cousins. One is perhaps the old aunt, his mother's sister, who Maimoun told us accompanies him when he travels because he is able to drink only the *hura* that she alone knows how to prepare.

We do not stay long. Beneath the protection of the roof, life is going forward like everywhere else. The children are being nursed and scolded and caressed. A young girl brings several *kwanos* on a tray, and when they are uncovered we are invited to have some stew and some beans. Water is passed in a bowl. But soon after we hear the call to prayer from the mosque next to the palace, we begin the greetings for farewell. We have shared their food and rested and now it is time to leave, time for the women to say their prayers. We retrace our steps through the shadowy rooms to the swallows who are still twittering beneath the arches, still swooping back and forth as they like from their nests in the *zaure* out into the bright sunlight.

And Aïssa, what about Aïssa, the friend I love? She is our friend in Kano, the one I stayed with overnight when I arrived a few weeks ago. We knew each other first in New York, where her husband was a student and she was a young woman with a baby, taking the subway downtown to sewing school. When I stayed with her and Ibrahim in Kano, they had six children. The sixth is a baby called Farid, only seven weeks old, and she carries him with her when she goes out. She takes me around Kano, the chauffeur driving us everywhere: here are the crenellated walls built in the twelfth century, here is one of the fourteen gates to the city, Kofar Rumfa, dating from the reign of Mohammed Rumfa, 1463–99. Here is the museum that shows us the piece of *tukunya* from the fifteenth century, *hulas* from the fourteenth exactly like the ones men wear today. And here is an old photograph of the British in Zaria sounding blank cannon in an open field to let the Hausas know the feel of a strong arm.

When we have looked at everything, Aïssa takes me to the house in the old city where she grew up. We have come to visit her grandmother, to show her the new baby. Aïssa's forty days are just past, the days when a woman attended by her mother and sisters remains in seclusion after childbirth, bathing with steaming water, scrubbing with neem branches. The chauffeur waits in the narrow street where the houses lean toward each other to shut out the sun. We enter through the *zaure* and Aïssa stops to show me the ledge where, in the days before there was electricity, a candle was set to light the way. We go through one room after another, each hung with embroidered cloth, arriving at last in a room where three old women are sitting together. We are greeted by cries of excitement and enthusiasm: here is Aïssa and here is her baby. We take off our sandals and sit down with them. The baby is passed from hand to hand, all the women exclaiming over him, all laughing in happiness: here is their own dear Aïssa, and here is her baby, here we all are, at last and forever.

When we are back in the car, I ask Aïssa which one was her grandmother; I hadn't been sure. The grandmother was the one in the middle, the others were her cowives. But Aïssa had grown up with all of them. They have known her all her life. The grandfather was long dead, he had died rather young. Now these three old women spend their days together, receiving visitors, saying their prayers, remembering the long life they have lived in common.

Next to Aïssa's house is the house where Ibrahim grew up and where his father, too, was a child. Ibrahim is twelve years older than Aïssa and remembers the day when she was born.

He remembers that he liked to hold her when she was a baby, to carry her everywhere. They married when she was fourteen. She has shown me the photograph taken the day after their wedding. They sit side by side, her face smooth as a child's. Ibrahim's eyes are melancholy, contained. They had lived in Ibrahim's house, and when later he takes us to greet his father and shows us the rooms where he and Aïssa spent their first months together, he says that the happiest moments of his life were passed between these walls. Aïssa had a child, they came to New York where another child was born, spent three years there, and then returned to Kano. Another child, then twins. Aïssa established a business from the house, designing clothes and selling them. She keeps the money she earns, it is her own.

Then one day Ibrahim told Aïssa he was thinking of taking a second wife. I laughed, she said, I thought he was joking. But when he mentioned it another day, she saw, incredulously, that he was serious. He had fallen in love with his secretary. No, she said, you cannot bring another woman into this house. I will not agree to it. It was resolved, finally, by Ibrahim's setting up a second household with his new wife. He spends two nights with Aïssa, two nights away. There is nothing casual about this arrangement. The cycle must be followed scrupulously. Money must be distributed exactly—gifts, servants, school fees.

Aïssa takes me to the Qur'an and opens it to the page that says it is permissible for a man to have up to four wives, if he is able to provide for them equally. This is the passage they all point to, she says. But the Prophet meant something quite different. It had to do with another time, when there were widows and unattended women who needed protection in times of war. Now, a man just takes a fancy to someone. And what are we to do? The children, according to Hausa custom, are in the man's custody. Can we leave them?

Later on, Aïssa asks me if I think it is possible for a man to treat two women exactly the same. We are standing in the court of her house, with its potted oleander and rose bushes. It is evening and the air is cool. I think for a minute and say I don't know. She says that if it is difficult to treat even two children exactly the same, how much more so two wives. When Ibrahim first told me about her, she says, I kept going over everything, wondering what had gone wrong, what I hadn't been able to give him. But do you know the worst of it? she asks. I've loved him all my life, and I do still. But I don't respect him as I once did.

Tonight we are alone, Ibrahim is with his other wife. We eat our dinner upstairs at a long dining-room table under a fan. A young girl, barefoot, a servant, carries the dishes up and down. Afterward we watch television for a while, the news of the day. The manager of the Bank of the North has been flown back from Germany, dead, where he had gone for an operation. There has been a gathering of ministers in Lagos. Then we watch a soap opera in Hausa. Modern young women and men with jobs and flats: *yan zamani.* Just before we turn the television off to go to bed, a woman comes on who demonstrates with the aid of a glass of water and a spoonful of sugar how to treat a child suffering from dehydration. This much water, this much sugar, given throughout the day and throughout the night. Then Aïssa leaves me and descends the outside stairs to her room below with its big bed and her cupboard of Pyrex dishes, graduated in size, her dowry, similar to Maimoun's cupboard of the humbler *kwano,* also arranged by size. Farid sleeps in a crib next to the bed.

I have been given a room off the large room upstairs with its sofas and chairs where we have been watching television. Prayer beads hang from the handle of the closet door. I fall instantly asleep beneath a large overhead fan. If I liked, I could have turned on the air conditioner. I hear nothing, dream nothing, until very early in the morning I am wakened by the first call to prayer. Allah, flung against a dark sky. The same call from another mosque, farther away, and then another, and another. One comes from so nearby it must be the *mu'azzin* of the little neighborhood mosque we could see from the court last evening, white pigeons swirling around its dome at twilight. For half an hour the cry is repeated again and again, thrilling, imperative. From below, there is the clink of a bucket; Aïssa is up making her ablutions. Prayer is better than sleep, and while I lie in bed, mute, all of Kano is rising to praise and to a plea for forgiveness.

Moon in Third Quarter

Sai an sha wuya a kan tuna Allah.
Only when you have endured suffering do you remember God.

One night Maimoun is already sitting with us outside Zara's house, Fasuma sprawled on her lap, when we hear El Gouni's clap at the gate. We have been passing Fasuma back and forth between us, trying to distract her from the piercing misery of a first tooth. Only a little more than a week ago, the night of the full moon, her gums were smooth, notched with tiny indentations where teeth would come. Now, in the middle of a smile, her face puckers and she jerks her head from side to side, the soft brush of her hair ruddy in the starlight. Her fingers clench to fists, battering the air, pushing away our hands and faces. We talk a little among ourselves but our attention is on Fasuma. In fact, it is clear Maimoun can scarcely think of anything else. If Zara or I are holding Fasuma when she begins to cry, Maimoun from politeness will wait a moment before she reaches out to take her. When we are talking, her eyes wander restlessly back to Fasuma.

"*Shigo!*" Zara calls out, and El Gouni enters through the gate. Zara is immediately on her feet, walking to meet her. El

Gouni comes forward out of the shadows, reaches out for Zara's hand, holds it tightly in her own. Her face opens in the smile I remember, the wide gums and straight white teeth. Unlike most women in Matameye, El Gouni goes uncoiffed. Her gray hair escapes from beneath her headscarf in tiny ringlets. I have stood as well, and with her free hand she reaches for mine. She is standing between us, between Zara and me, a hand in each of ours. Helplessly, I am jealous again of El Gouni, of Zara's other mother, the one she may yet love more. El Gouni is looking from one of us to the other, as if taking her bearings. Then she looks down at Maimoun, greets her on Fasuma, on the children at home.

This time she sits in the chair that Zara has just vacated, and it is Zara who sits on the hard slats of the Hausa bed. Greetings over, El Gouni's face assumes a look of sorrow so profound the night seems to open around us. The sky is deep with stars. The neem tree stands shadowless in the sand. The moon will rise late over the roof tonight, perhaps when we are already sleeping.

Marianma is not coming. At least not this week or next. She may come later, at harvest, but she is not ready to make the trip at this time. El Gouni received word today. Someone from the village where Marianma lives with her husband brought the message this afternoon, just as she was finishing her prayers. At first glance she thought the messenger was Marianma herself. She saw only his shadow in the *zaure*, and she has looked for Marianma's arrival so often, night and day, that of course it seemed to her that the shadow might belong to Marianma herself. But no. This was a young man who was coming to Matameye to deliver some money to his sister and so had brought the message. He had told her that Marianma would come as soon as she could and then he had left. That was all. But her own sadness, El Gouni said, lifting her gaze to each of ours, was great.

Zara lowers her head, pressing her hands together in front of her. *Assha, Assha,* she croons, just as in Hadiza's hut she had done when the old woman related the death of her daughter in childbirth. Oh, *Assha.* Her hair falls forward over her face, a veil of sorrow. For the moment, there is nothing to be said.

But Maimoun, Fasuma hoisted over one shoulder, is shaking her head, sucking on her teeth. She is angry and so am I. Why should Marianma not have come to visit El Gouni? Why should the shadow in the *zaure* have been a stranger's instead of hers? And why should her babies have died in the first place? Why should these things have happened? And with my anger is washed away all jealousy of El Gouni, my fear that she will replace me as Zara's mother.

El Gouni is bent over the string bag she is carrying and is drawing from it what seems to be a piece of white cotton folded into squares. With careful fingers she opens it, section by section, then shakes it out, holding it up by the top corners a little away from her face. "But do you see what Marianma has sent me?" she asks. We can see nothing, only a white flag suspended in the night with what look like bits of color flung across it.

Then, turning it slowly around, she lowers the cloth and smoothes it over her knees. What rises to meet us is a peacock embroidered in shimmering colors: pale blue verging on frost, glossy black, lemon, and a deep watery aquamarine. His tail is lifted behind his head like the risen sun, but the lunar eyes are misty.

Zara is leaning forward toward El Gouni and has taken the edge of the cloth in her fingers. Immediately, with the shift in light, the colors change; the silvery blue is thrown into shadow, the black throws off a lustrous sheen. We are speechless with wonder. Who could this Marianma be who has been able to imagine such a thing?

"We chased them, when we were little," Maimoun says,

and I remember that she played with Marianma when they were children, that together they plunged their arms into the sand in the effort to reach water.

From bending over the cloth, Zara looks up quickly at Maimoun as if she had forgotten this fact herself. "Oh, the peacocks," she murmurs. Then, turning back, tracing the peacock's tail with her finger, Zara asks a question for which my anger should have prepared me, but which nonetheless takes me by surprise. "But why, El Gouni?" she asks, her eyes on the embroidery, and pauses so long I know she is uncertain what it is she wants to say. "Why do you think Marianma has had to suffer so much?"

Fasuma has begun to cry, sharp, piercing screams, and Maimoun gets up and walks up and down with her. It is clear that Maimoun is losing patience, that she would like to have a moment to listen to the night, to listen to El Gouni, so I get up and take Fasuma, who snuffles and wheezes and at last is quiet. But it is not until we are sitting down again, Fasuma lying on her back on my lap, that she is silent. Her little hennaed feet are resting in my hands, the silky flats of her feet, and I think of Zara's bare heels on the road to Kantché, how exposed they had been riding on either side of the burning motor of the mobylette, perched above the flying road beneath.

El Gouni has said nothing at all. The neem tree is perfectly still, no breeze or stir of air. But the leaves revolve in still concentric circles, like iron filings round a magnet; the design itself is in motion, whirling round a point. Beyond, although it too looks so still, the north star is steadily circling the pole.

"At first I thought it was because she fell into the fire," El Gouni begins, her eyes on the ground in front of her. She is silent for a moment and then continues, her voice low. "She was very little and didn't know any better. I was arguing with my cowife, I wasn't watching." She pauses again. "But her screams were terrible."

With these words, her hands that were lying flat on her thighs coil into fists. Then she takes a breath and looks around at us. "I used to think that was why."

Zara responds eagerly, spontaneously, seizing one of El Gouni's hands. "Of course that's not why. Of course not," she says, smoothing the fist flat. She looks around for agreement from Maimoun and myself. But we say nothing.

"No, I don't think so, either," El Gouni replies, letting go of Zara's hand and, sitting up straight in her chair, stroking the piece of cloth on her lap. She moves her legs slightly to one side and again the peacock shimmers, sending out sparks of light. The starlight is playing on Zara's face, on El Gouni's face and Maimoun's, and although I cannot see it, on mine. We too must be sending out sparks of light, must be reflecting our own dark surfaces.

"Then I believed," El Gouni continues, "that Marianma's suffering had to do with the midwives. That the babies had been injured during their deliveries. That if the midwives had known what to do, the babies would not have died. But," El Gouni finishes, "I soon came to see that Marianma's fate was too unusual to be explained away so easily."

El Gouni's eyes are fixed on her lap, on the naked white edge of the cloth resting on her thighs. She cannot see the peacock hanging like an emblem in the night. But before our eyes, it refuses to remain still. At one moment its shimmering tail is throwing off the radiance of the sun, a flame so bright the intricately worked pattern is consumed. At another it seems to cast a light like the moon's in which shapes and angles hidden at noonday throw deep shadows. Is it Marianma's sorrow, I wonder, that has opened her eyes to the peacock? Or the stab of joy, piercing and fleet, she knew the first time she looked on the face of a baby? Or had she been dazzled even as a little girl, playing in the sand, when she had looked up and seen above her the wide spread of the peacock's tail?

"It was only later," El Gouni continues, her hands resting on the edge of the cloth, "much later, after the healers had all been called and after the Centre had arranged for the pills from the hospital, that I came to see things differently. Then, finally, I realized that if there was no single thing that could be done to take away Marianma's suffering, then probably there was no single reason for it, either. That sounds simple, I know, but it is not. If I could not release Marianma from her pain, if the lost babies could not be restored, then I knew I must embrace Marianma as one who suffers. But as one, too," she says, slowly folding the peacock away, removing it from our gaze, "who has received the gift of sight."

She bends down and returns the white cloth to her string bag.

"I saw that there was no explanation for Marianma's sufferings," El Gouni says after a moment, hands flat on her thighs, "except that Allah had allowed them. It was a matter of choosing what was given."

Zara has been listening attentively to El Gouni. I cannot tell from her face what she thinks. And Maimoun is already on her feet, bending to lift Fasuma into her own arms.

"In any case," El Gouni concludes, "I pray for the peace that Allah gives."

Then, abruptly changing the subject, looking around from one of us to another, she tells us that last night she dreamed of her mother. Her father, she says, was ninety-seven when she was born. Yes, it's true, he was an old man and died immediately after. But her mother, that was another story. Sometimes she dreams about her still. There she is, spooning out the *tuwo*, handing a bowl to El Gouni. In the dream, she says, looking at me, her mother is still young, maybe like Maimoun and Zara. And she herself is barefoot, with a little piece of pink yarn tied around her ankle.

"Tell her, Zara," I say, turning to her in the dark, speaking in English, "because for these things I can't speak. Tell her that I, too, dream about my mother. I see her standing in a garden. She is holding me in her arms and looking at me so gladly."

"Oh, but that's paradise," El Gouni responds, smiling at me. "You know that when we die we awake in a garden flowing with milk and honey. We find there, resting in the shade, all the ones we have lost."

But in the meantime? I want to ask her. What are we to do? How are we to live?

That night, waking before dawn to the sound of the Qur'anic students' chant, I don't know if I have been dreaming of Ben Waleru or of my mother. My mother's eyes are green and reflect the light that falls on bush and tree. But there Ben stands in a garden spiky with lotus buds and bird of paradise, his arms around Zara. Or is it Patience he is holding, born only days before Zara, his own baby girl, his fifth child, the one who when the rains began wore pink knitted booties and a sweater to match? Dead in the Biafran war. The frangipani tree is heavy with white blossoms.

Below the monotonous sound of the chanting, below the to and fro that follows the same antiphonal tides as the prayers of my childhood, there is another sound, hard to place. A low boom, perhaps the play of electricity sparked by unimaginable collisions somewhere in the atmosphere. It comes from below, but also from above, from far above the house, from the depths of a vast sky that even now is preparing to fill with light. The earth will soon be swinging into the sun and the shadows that have sheltered us tonight will disappear like waves running out on sand. To the north stretches the largest desert on earth.

On the other side of the wall, El Gouni is making her ablutions. There is the clink of a bucket, then the raucous scream of a rooster. The peacocks are stirring in the *gawo* trees. She is washing her face from ear to ear, from forehead to chin, then her hands and forearms, and last her feet. Not forgetting the space between each toe. In a moment she will reach down a clean *pagne* from the palm tree in her compound that serves as a cupboard: clothes hang from the tough fronds of the trunk, ladles, a strainer, even an iron pot. El Gouni is an indifferent housekeeper, her mind is on other things. She is learning to read Arabic script. She ponders the embroidered peacock. In the late afternoon she sits with Zara, listening to her recount stories of the day.

But when she prays, what does she do?

Sa zuciya ga ci, shi ya kawo jin yunwa.
It is setting the heart on eating that brings on hunger.

How to speak to the silences, the spaces between?

It is not one night, waking to the chi-chi-chi of cicadas, the monotonous sound of seeds shaken in a pod, not one day, not one week, that the faces rise and hang for a moment in the air. It is rather every instant, waking or dreaming, that they ride at my back. They are there for the looking, biding their time.

There is a man holding up a line and a hook. His hair and eyelashes are white with brine, his teeth are black. The hook is sharp as the man's need but he seems scarcely to notice there is no fish. His eyes gaze past the hook to the extreme point of his longing, out past the Aran Islands to that point where vision is lost in a dazzle of mist. It is clear he would give up all he has for one moment of ease, and that he no longer holds out the least hope. He is past everything, past the impulse to shake his fist at the sky, past even the stammering attempt to speak. He has long ago forgotten the name and shape of what he cannot do without. If it were offered to him he might not have the sense to know, the strength to reach out his hand.

Another face, a woman's, appears beneath a dark woolen shawl. Her eyes are blue and have a wandering, watery look. At first glance you might think this woman foolish, absent-

minded to the last degree. She scarcely seems capable of fixing her attention for more than an instant, of cherishing the
slightest wish. But a second glance makes plain she wears that
air of distraction precisely to disguise the fact she thinks of
one thing, day and night. It can seem a matter of shame, a
hunger as desperate as this. She is sick with desire, she cannot
help herself. It is a case of someone lost to the world. But for
what is she starved? A turnip? The face of God? A caress?

There is too much in a single day, a superfluity that dulls
the senses. What are we to do with it all, the sun breaking on
roof and sand, the footstep in the street, the silver flash of a
bird's wing? Nor is it today alone—every day the same, if not
the sun, then wind scattering leaves against a wall, a clap of
thunder in the east. All this before a word is spoken, before
there is any question of reply. There is both too much and
much, much too little. And what we have, the brimming world
itself, does not always include the indispensable potato, rotting in the field.

Ciwon ido sai hak'uri.
With a malady of the eyes, have patience.

One night, only a week before I am to leave to return home, I ask Zara what has become of the child swaying on the scale in Matameye. Sometimes, without warning, his face appears, the weary eyes touching each of us in turn, the death grin, the forehead in its awful candor. But something else as well: a hole in his face, a hole reaching to the cheekbone. It must have been clearly visible from the start, but only now does it swim to the surface unchecked. She tells me that cavities like this one are the work of a bacterial infection called noma, not uncommon among such children. Then she says that he has not returned to the clinic, that his mother has probably taken him back to her village to die.

We are sitting outside, as usual, under the stars. It is late. The Qur'anic students, who most nights appear at the gate begging for food in the name of Allah, have received their bowl of *tuwo*, have silently eaten, and have gone their way. They are learning to live at the mercy of others and leave only their blessings behind: A*llah ya ba ɗa sa'a.*

In Zara's compound, certainly, there is no lack of food. Ever since my arrival the kitchen has been gradually filling. There is a bowl of eggs, the bottle of peanut oil El Gouni gave us, and a new loaf of bread. There is also a pot of rice and a tiny feathered pigeon. On the shelf beside the plastic mugs sits the bag of potatoes sent by Maimoun's sister, Koubra, and some ripe guavas. And from Amina, a bag of couscous carried from Kantché on the mobylette. There is also a pile of *cuku*, the dry Fulani cheese cut into rippled wedges, and beside it, carefully covered, a sliver of goat's meat.

This afternoon the gate scraped open and an old man came forward, bowing, knocking his chest with his fist. *Tsoho*, Zara called him: old man. He sank to his heels, a courtesy that must have come naturally to another generation, and Zara and I sank to ours. Squatting in the sand, we faced each other, no one in a position to look down on anyone else. He had brought something wrapped in brown paper and Zara cupped her hands to receive it. When she folded back the paper, flies had settled on a glistening piece of liver: taken, he told us, from a goat killed that morning. Zara thanked him, explaining that we would cook it with onions.

In fact, the kitchen is overflowing. All day long children arrive, sent by their parents with things for us to eat. This morning, two little girls stood at the screened door, each with an enamel tray bearing a covered *kwano* balanced on her head. When I held the door open they stepped inside, one after the other, lifting the trays from their heads. *Sannu 'yammata:* a word on which the lips close, a momentary hum that relishes the hoops in their ears, the pattern of henna around the soles of their feet, the flaps of cloth that have fallen over one ear. They watched as I removed the covers: *Benin tuwo* in one *kwano*, pepper sauce in the other. Then I had gone to the fridge and poured water from the gin bottle into the plastic mugs. They drank, holding the mugs in both hands, tilting their heads back for the last drop. "*Mun gode*," they said, we thank you, and, winding their headcloths into cushioning rings, lifting the trays back into place, had walked back out into the sun.

"But why?" I ask Zara. "Why so much?"

She tells me that here they say the stranger is your God. I am Zara's guest, her mother, and Matameye is seeing to it that she has the means to feed me.

"Yes," Zara says, clasping her hands together in her lap, "along with the breakdown of mucous membranes in the mouth, nose, and vagina, the sores and bleeding that follow, these cavities, too, are common. The starved flesh is itself eaten away."

"It's hard to take in," I say. "It's as if it becomes real only a little at a time."

"I know," Zara says. "At first I was so frightened I didn't know if I could learn to do anything. I just wanted to leave and go somewhere else. Now it's no less horrifying but I'm not so frightened. Of myself, I mean. Of turning away. But sometimes I wake up at night," and here she pauses, her face down, "I wake up, you know, and find I've been crying in my sleep."

"And yet, Zara," I say, wanting to change the subject, even now afraid of her sorrow, afraid she'll tell me something I can't bear to hear, "sometimes I think I've never seen you so happy as you are now, so completely at home."

"I think that's because I was a child here," Zara says, turning to look at me. "It's a place I remember. In some timeless way it seems completely familiar. That makes a great difference."

Zara is wearing a dress tonight, not a *pagne;* a green and white wax print, cut off at the knees, with a neck embroidered with white thread. She has already told me the man at the sewing machine we passed the night of the full moon, on our way to Maimoun's, made it for her.

"Yes, I can see it would make a difference," I reply. "Do you think of it often, the year we spent in Zinder when you were little?"

"Oh yes, often." Zara says. "At least at first I did. But the longer I'm here the more it all runs together, as if there weren't all those years between. As if the child I was then has become more and more the person I am now."

The Milky Way stands out like a bright mist in a sky of teeming blue; a single sweep, flowing from above the fluted edge of the tin roof and vanishing beyond the wall.

"Do you remember, Zara," I ask, "the day we went up to Zinder, you know, when we were sitting in the hostel, before we'd seen the house, do you remember you asked me about your sixth birthday?"

Zara is completely still. Her white legs gleam in the dark. Her hands are hanging loose over the iron armrests of the chair.

"I remember," she says after a moment. "I remember very well. I was afraid to see the house. The minute we got off the *taxi brousse* that morning I was afraid, even though the other times I'd been to Zinder, by myself, I'd never given it a thought. Even when I'd gone looking for the house."

"It was because I was there," I say.

"Yes," Zara answers, agreeing quickly. "That was it. Your presence made the difference. I think I can tell you about it now. You'd only just arrived then, you'd only been in Matameye a few days, so we really hadn't had any time together. And when we arrived in Zinder I remembered my birthday so vividly, I was afraid. And maybe angry, a little, too. It all seemed too much."

"And when you saw the house?"

"It was nothing, nothing at all," she says and pauses. "It was the memory itself that had me in its grip. The house looked like any other house. It seemed to have nothing to do with what I remembered."

I am glad Zara is taking her time because my heart is beating fast.

"Tell me," I say at last.

"Oh, it will probably sound like nothing. Or maybe not, I don't know." She pauses again, then begins speaking rapidly. "It was just that when Lizzy and I were at Mme. Renault's that day I started to imagine how it would be when we got home. You know, because it was my birthday. I think I'd already seen you when we got up in the morning, you were lying in bed, coughing and coughing, but sometime later, at Mme. Renault's—she was being so gentle with me and all the children were singing 'Joyeuse Anniversaire' and Lizzy was so excited—I started to imagine that when I got home at noon you'd be up, waiting for me, that—I think this is the way I imagined it, although it sounds odd to say it out loud—that you'd have put your sickness aside for me, because it was my birthday, that's the way I was thinking about it, and that you'd be waiting for me there on the veranda."

"But that didn't happen, did it?" I say.

"Well, of course you couldn't help it," Zara says. "You were sick. I know that."

The starlight is shining on the neem leaves, making bright the entire compound.

"It was just this," Zara says, beginning to speak in a rush. "Someone brought us home from school and we ran in through the gate. The veranda I think must have been in shadow, because at first I thought I saw you there, just as I had imagined, waiting for me. The picture was so clear to me. But then when I got closer, I saw it wasn't you at all. It wasn't anyone. Just some flowers in a pot."

Zara stops short, and this time is silent so long I wonder if she thinks I'm listening. "Yes," I say. "We did have some flowers like that."

"But that wasn't it," she says, speaking more slowly now, her face tilted toward the sky. "Of course I was disappointed that you weren't on the veranda as I had wanted you to be. Terribly disappointed. But it wasn't that. Not really. It was that when I went to find you, in the room where you were—"

Here Zara breaks off and turns in the dark to ask me a question. I see that Zara's eyes look baffled and afraid, as mine must look to her as well.

"Was there a little thing to stand on, at the doorway to the room? You know, when you came in from the veranda?"

"A ledge," I say. "A kind of raised place so that you could shut the door tightly at night."

"Yes," she says, turning her face away again, back to the sky. "A ledge. That's what I remember. I was standing on it, looking into the room. You were lying in bed, and there was a glass of water there on the floor, with flies around the rim. Black flies. I thought, I'll go to her anyway, she'll be glad to see me, it's my birthday. She's probably been waiting for me all morning. Just as I've been waiting. But when I got closer—" And here Zara stops again and, taking her hands from the armrests that she has been clasping tightly, holds onto her elbows.

"It was that you didn't seem to know who I was," Zara says, turning to me with tears in her eyes. "You didn't even seem to know me at all. And what was so scary was that after a moment I didn't recognize you either. It was as if you'd turned into a complete stranger."

I reach across the space between us for Zara's hand and hold on to it.

"It was that your eyes looked all unhinged and distracted," she continues. "As if you were looking straight through me to something else. I know now it must have been the fever. But you might as well have been looking at the moon."

"Oh, Zara," I say, after a moment, still holding her hand. "Why didn't you ever tell me?"

And suddenly I see that I have known all this from the beginning, the periwinkles blooming in a line of red clay pots, the glass of water ringed with flies, the flat wash of light playing on the shoulders of the child standing on the ledge, in the doorway, have known and seen it all about to happen—have been that child myself—and known, too, that there was nothing, in time or out of it, that I or anyone else could have done to have stayed the blow.

We sit still for a minute, looking at each other, saying nothing. There is only the steady, monotonous rattle of cicadas filling the spaces between us, filling the night that on every side is opening around us. Unwittingly, Zara has told me what I have long suspected: that fever or no fever, however she may excuse me on grounds of illness, it's been what I have chosen to call my inattention, my preoccupation with shadows, that at times has made us unrecognizable to each other. While I was lost in my own wanderings, pursuing fleeting fragments of memory and desire, her eyes were on me, a creature whose gaze looked straight through her, a creature who certainly could not be called her mother. And this, too, I now see—because of who I am, because of all that happened to others before I was born, that happened blindly to me—could not have been otherwise.

"I wish things had been different," I say at last, "that you might have been spared all this."

And then Zara, before releasing my hand, quickly raises it to her cheek.

Our heads against the backs of our chairs, we can see individual stars, some very bright, others more faint, and then behind them a cloudy light, fathomless, that seems to be moving backward through space. The luminous band of the Milky Way turns like a wheel in the sky, and it is only the dark body of the earth, the horizons cutting off what lies beyond, that prevent our seeing the great swish of revolving light. Even now, sitting beside me, Zara is making her way, traveling through the spaces of her childhood into a future where I, along with all those who came before me, will take my place in the unreachable past.

"You know, don't you," I say, a few minutes later, "the first thing you ever gave me?" I am thinking of Africa, how it is here that Zara was born, here that we lost each other for a time, and here, just now, that she has given me her latest, most luminous, gift.

She nods, having heard the story so many times before, how when she was six weeks old a gift dropped from her hand into mine. It was in Lagos, at Bar beach with its terrific undertow, its fringe of pines and lofty, royal palms. The Bay of Biscay—what old atlases called the slave coast. Fishermen were bringing in their boats on one long, high surge after another, dredging up the day's catch—sardines, barracuda, prawns—and pouring it all in one slippery rush into the buckets of market women waiting on the beach. Mike had carried Zara down to the water's edge. Standing there in white shorts, the waves rushing up to his knees and funneling out again, he seemed to be moving along the horizon himself. With one arm he held Zara against his chest; with the other pointed out to her lolling head the orange sun falling into the water, the screaming, diving gulls. Then he stooped, picked up something from the sand, and turned. Tossing his head like a horse, pawing the sand, he galloped up the beach to where I sat. "Now," he said, coming to a stop. "You can give it to her now." And leaning down pried open Zara's baby fist. Straight into my hand, a tiny coiled seashell.

"I used to think you were trying to give me what I needed so badly, I don't know, not patience exactly; endurance, something like that," I say, imagining the way the shell must once have rolled unresisting on the floor of the ocean. How it had turned over and over, lifting against the sand, until its silky whorls had come to rest in her own silky palm. "Do you think that has anything to do with what El Gouni was talking about the other night, about accepting Marianma as one who suffers?"

"Yes," Zara says quickly, surprising me, because I understand so little, myself, what I mean. It is very late and the quarter moon is rising over the house, throwing a sudden sheen on the roof; a moon with its top lopped off, but full and pregnant below, a cradle rocking.

"You hear about that all the time," she continues, after a moment. *"Sai bak'uri.* Have patience. Like when we were at Maimoun's the other night. I asked Sani why so many people lost seed by planting early, and he said it was because they lacked *bak'uri,* because they couldn't wait until the rains had started. Or if a child dies, people say that to the parents. *Sai bak'uri."*

Somewhere a dog has begun to bark, a long, gliding howl. Another dog joins in, and then another.

"Is it to surrender to things?" I ask.

"Not exactly," she says. "No, I don't think so. Or at least not in a passive way. It's said to beggars, too, when you have nothing to give. *Sai bak'uri.* Wait. But here that's considered doing something in itself. I don't know if El Gouni accepts Marianma's suffering. But she waits, she prays. She asks for understanding. She said to me once that in prayer asking and responding are the same thing, there isn't any difference."

The neem tree, the front of the house, our faces, are all moving into moonlight. The Milky Way, on the other hand, looks farther away, less distinct.

"It is that I would still like to find," I say. "The patience, the belief, whatever it takes, to ask, to respond. But here, during this time with you, I have found, without even asking, what I had most hoped for."

We sit for a few moments in silence, watching the dark shadow of the wall beginning to emerge on the sand. There is no need to explain. "And you, Zara," I ask at last, "during these years you have spent here in Matameye. What is it that you have found?"

"Joy," she says.

PART III ZINDER

Zuciyar mutum birninsa.
The human heart is where we live: a walled city.

Travelers leaving Matameye south along a shaded avenue of neems abruptly find themselves with nothing overhead except the unleashed sky, immense and still. On either side, the land rushes toward the horizon, disappearing at last only because the eye fails, the earth curves away. Here and there a tree startles up or a dusty field of millet. But in a landscape as vast as this one, they vanish into thin air. The baobab spins lunatic in space, the acacia falls off into nowhere. It is the same with the *birnin kaouri*, villages in the bush, floating on the horizon within their gleaming enclosures of straw. Some are only hazy vapors in the distance, pointed roofs lost against a white blaze of sky. Villages close to the road are another matter; they swim past announced: Tsaduni, Soma, Da'din Kowa. Twenty-six kilometers later, before anyone passing through is aware of a change in a landscape shifting from dusty dry to savanna, another sign appears: *Frontière Nigeria,* the border closed by the British more than fifty years ago to protest the Vichy sympathies of the colonial government, Afrique Occidentale Française.

A crossbar, balanced between two iron poles stuck in the sand, is lifted to allow a car to pass. People on foot go round. The low building on one side of the bar is cooled by louvered shutters, hinged at the top and propped open from below with sticks. Inside, the forms shoved across the desk are in French. The men in uniform sitting behind the desk are smoking Gauloises. On the other side of the bar, in a building just like the other, windows open out in small metal frames, and the forms are in English. The officials are smoking Rothmans. And yet, despite all this, despite the imported cigarettes and languages, the windows and bottled water, no one is speaking anything but Hausa. The roosters are strutting, the money changers are waiting at their tables beneath the neems. Children, balancing trays of *goro* nuts on their heads, walk back and forth past Fulani women who peddle milk in calabashes scorched with figures of lizards and cows. On either side the prayer grounds are spread with mats of golden straw.

As the road continues south to Kano, it passes almost immediately through the town of Daura where the Hausa state was born when Bayejida seized Queen Daura's throne by killing a sacred snake with his sword. Soon after Daura, with its palace of arches and columns, of lofty vaults and filtered light, the flat land gradually turns from sand to soil. Mango trees spring up and Abyssinian rollers loop and tumble on blue wings. The sky leans close to the earth. By the time Kano is in sight, the desert has been all but left behind. Eucalyptus groves make shade during even the hottest part of the day and the white dome of the Emir's mosque rises from the leafy tops of locust trees. The soil is red. At twilight, goats standing on the dusty remains of the city walls look out over fields of ripening maize.

After leaving Kaduna, the last of Hausaland, the road in its plunge away from the desert veers west as well as south, because it must cross the Niger River which is sweeping headlong, southeast, down to the vast conflux of tributaries that empty into the Gulf of Guinea. The road, measured now in miles, continues through savanna, but the land through which it cuts is little by little overrun by a dense tangle of trunks and fronds. Seven hundred miles later, Lagos is in sight. Here black mambas can be seen twisting across the road, and the forest on either side is dark with hanging vines and butterflies.

That is one road, the road running south. It finally comes to a stop at the coast, where coconut palms and pines drop off into the churning waters of the Atlantic.

The other road leading out of Matameye, also for a short distance an avenue of neems, runs north. It passes through Kantché and on up to Takieta, where it joins the Route Nationale flowing east on its way to Lake Chad, passing through Zinder, Goure, and Goudoumaria. The sign in Matameye gives eighty-seven kilometers as the distance to Zinder. Only about thirty of those, the stretch to Takieta, point due north. But on that road, the road from Matameye to Zinder, the land spectacularly gives way to desert. Ten kilometers out, there is no longer any place to hide. The sky pounds white. Trees fall away, the brush turns sparse and spiky. Only the blind can ignore the sand breaking in broad waves through the scruffy brush. What else is there to see? A camel nibbling a thorn bush. Light on light, pressed against closed eyelids. The imagination reels off and away, trying to remember the feel of shadows and night. For an instant, all roads are forgotten: the road of yesterday vanishing south to the Bight of Benin; the road of tomorrow flung further and further into the desert; even the road of today, rushing always and at last to Zinder, city of winds and wheeling vultures, of rocks shimmering in the heat. All forgotten, in some reverie of still cool waters waiting in darkness.

And yet—and here is the contradiction, the source of all the torment and delight—in that single moment, endless, one is aware only that this gaze of intolerable light, blistering, brutal, is the most one has ever known of joy.

First Call to Prayer: *Fajr*

Early one morning, startling out of sleep at the shrill cry of the *mu'azzin*, I decide to go up to Zinder and return that evening. I am to leave Matameye in three days, to return to New York, and I would like before I go to leave some treats for Zara. The lost birthday doll, the one she doesn't remember receiving for her sixth birthday, haunts me. Late as it is, I must not think it is too late, because I decide to look for something even now that would soothe and delight, something from Zinder, perhaps something from Michel's where we had once seen the trembling kitten: chocolate, cheese, a box or two of Petits Beurres. That is how I find myself beside a window on a *taxi brousse*, black leather bag flat on my knees, sweeping between the rows of neems and out onto the road with its glimpse of burning day. The roof of the taxi cuts off all except a margin of sky, but the land beyond the open window extends level as a wing. And there is a hole in the floor of the taxi, between my feet and those of the woman sitting next to me, to let in the road rushing beneath.

Like myself, the woman is wearing flip-flops, but on her knees, instead of a leather bag with a blue water canteen inside, sits a small child whose eyes slid shut as soon as the taxi lurched into motion. Three tiny leather pouches, amulets stitched inside, slowly rise and fall on his chest. His arms are frail; in fact, they are much too frail. Did she place the amulets there to protect him from hunger? And if she had not done so, would she have blamed herself for negligence?

I am turning over these questions when it occurs to me that parental guilt is not, after all, about the child falling into the fire, the lime that is found too late. No, *koumia* has to do with the shame brought on like a fever by bringing a child into a world one already knows is gravid with suffering. The child will suffer, that is certain, and by giving birth one has allowed that this should happen.

On her other side, next to the window, a man wearing a white hat, a *hula* embroidered with blue thread, holds himself stiffly upright. He is staring straight ahead, watching the road through the windshield that frames the driver's head. On the dashboard, raised for the passengers' attention, is a sticker:

> *Entre Nous Patience*
> *Qui Sait Sauf Allah.*

There is silence in the taxi. The sun on the roof of the taxi burns hot. A short time ago, while we were still waiting in the *auto gare* in Matameye, the woman beside me called out for the driver to start; it was hot and the babies were crying. Through the open windows, now, the wind whirls dust in our faces, scalding our skin. In the row behind us sits an old man whose head is wound in a black turban. His face is deeply lined, his eyes fixed steadfastly on some point in the landscape that is replaced by another and another. When the sign for Kantché appears by the side of the road and is left behind, he doesn't appear to notice. The old man's turban protects his hair and neck; the women are wearing headcloths, and, at the other window, the white embroidered *hula* remains steadily in place.

It is only my hair that is flying around my head like a demon's, whipping across my eyes and mouth. The hands resting on my black leather bag are no color at all. They look as if they have been drained of something, as if by some terrible calamity the color had all been bleached out of them and they are waiting for a cure.

In the distance a gust of sand moves quickly along like a rising wave that swells before it breaks. It blows higher and higher, spume flying, is beginning to fade against the sky, is disappearing into larger regions of light, when suddenly the man in the black turban calls out sharply to the driver. The taxi swerves to the side of the road and spins to a stop against a spray of sand. On the immense landscape, there is no village in sight. The old man gathers his robes and steps down, swinging the sliding door shut behind him. As he chops off into the brush beneath the blazing sun, we can see he is wearing only one flip-flop. His other foot is bare. Then the hole in the floor of the taxi changes from a patch of sand to a flowing stream of tar, and looking back we see a black turban and fluttering gown receding against the sand. Soon these are blotted out by the sticker in the rear window:

Komai na Allah ne.
Everything comes from Allah.

Where the old man vanishes, a flock of egrets, wheeling sharply, flashes white above the brown earth. Or would you call it sand? A widening expanse of sand with low brush scattered over it and dwindling plots of millet.

But already, falling from a trance of rushing air and swirling dust, we are nearing Takieta, the sign approaches and is left behind, and the taxi comes to a stop in front of a stand where a vendor is selling soap and cigarettes, white candles wrapped in blue paper. The child leaning against the woman next to me has been sleeping soundly. Now his eyes fly open and immediately close, his feet, dangling from legs thin as sticks, twitch nervously. He takes a long shuddering breath, then settles back into sleep.

One arm on the wheel, the driver leans across the front seat and asks the vendor if he knows where Hamid is staying, the man he brought down from Zinder a week ago, the one who said he'd want to return. The vendor begins to answer but his words are lost in the chant of a blind beggar who is coming toward us, leaning on a stick. He stands in the window, mouth wide open on teeth stained orange with *goro*. Face tilted to our gaze, in a strong, quavering voice he sings his prayer of supplication. Unsure what to do, I tell myself I am saving my money for Zara's treat, but the woman beside me takes her hand from the child's knees and unwinds a knot in her *pagne*. Then she reaches across me to drop a coin in his bowl. With her gesture I am reminded of the words of the Prophet: "O A'isha! Do not turn the poor away without giving if but half a date!"

"*Allah ya ba ∂a sa'a,*" the blind beggar murmurs at the sound of the clink, his grip loosening on the stick worn smooth with handling. May Allah give you good fortune.

"*Allah ya sa,*" she replies: may He do so.

Good fortune to her and to her sleeping child, to the vendor with his elbows on the window, and to the old man who may still be striding one foot bare over the burning sand. Good fortune to the taxi at large. To all who give and to all who do not.

The hole in the floor of the taxi again swirls from sand to tarmac, but we are no longer traveling due north. At Takieta the taxi has picked up the Route Nationale and is now moving more east than north, the final fifty-two kilometers to Zinder. We are sitting motionless, the woman with her sleeping child and myself, feet at rest in flip-flops. It is the road itself that is taking us west to east, into the harsh light of day. A procession of pale cattle is drifting toward us, great horns curved like lyres, heads humbly down, hooves lost in a light shuffle. Riding their backs, pecking in the clouds of dust lifting from their path, are snowy egrets, very white.

A young man approaches in a broad Fulani hat, a circle of fine braids hanging to his shoulders beneath the brim. He stops as we pass, his gaze firm, one hand raised in greeting. I think of Zara's story: how she had been traveling with a group of American friends, and when the car had had a flat some Fulani herders had come out of the fields. They had all stared at each other in silence, all about the same age, young men, young women, had forgotten everything, tires, cattle, their new dignity as adults. On both sides had dropped all pretense of indifference, had stood close to one another, unabashed as small children, staring their fill, until someone, on one side or the other, overcome with curiosity, had reached out a hand to touch an earring, a lock of hair.

But now he is gone, the Fulani of today, and out the window, unmistakably, the tide of sand is rising. The bright, occasional patches of millet are going under. And this is the rainy season, as green as it gets. Seventeen years ago, during the harmattan, on the way to Niamey by way of Dosso, when we had first crossed paths with the old woman in Hadiza's hut, the wind had been pressing the spiky bushes to the ground: nothing but browns and whitened grays and tawny yellows. As far as one looked, every reed and branch stripped by sand to its essential loneliness.

But the *gawo*, oh the *gawo* had been in leaf, even then. Perversely blooming according to a law of its own. Those tiny

platelets, so fine, green like frost. You might have been looking at a patch of fog: and then there had been the tree, the lacy
gawo, a vapor caught in its branches. On the immense land it
had seemed to move forward to meet us, its tiny leaves trembling in delight. As if its garden branches, blossoming there on
the desert waste, were held out to remind us that rapture was
the deepest thing of all, deeper than pain and longing, deeper
even than death.

And now, in a season when everything else is doing its
best to come to leaf, the stubborn *gawo* remains dry as a stick.
Of all the trees that are in the wood, a prickly wreath of woe.
Gawo ka k'iya ruwan Allah, the saying goes. *Gawo*, you've
refused the water sent by God. But beneath its stricken limbs,
millet plants will flourish as they will not beneath any other's
because here no shade blocks their growth. And the *gawo* is
hospitable to shaggy nests, to tufted birds with orange legs
leaping from its branches into thin air.

Sannu Tsohuwa: that is how I am seen. My teeth are crumbling, my hands, resting here on the black leather bag, are
blanched and dry. Almonds, shot from their pods. And yet it
stirs me, all this, as it did before: the heat shimmering just
above the ground, the wavering forms stilled for a moment in
their passage. In this spot, of all others, where space opens
toward infinity, the arc of longing rises pure against the sky.
Hunger leaping like a flame. I want! I want! The ladder narrowing toward the moon. And here, too, along this road, the
old question looking out from the air. The question on which
life itself depends, waking one in the night to a pounding
heart. But what? For an instant—it is only that, and yet it is
everything—the question disengages itself from bush and tree.
Stares out from the immense silence of space. Oh what? And
then the terror as it slips away. Lost because the bird will not
stay put, the taxi rushes on.

The little boy sleeping on her lap has begun to stir. He digs his head into her breasts, then stretches his legs, toes pointing in. When he looks around and catches my eye, he curls up again, thumb in his mouth, and I suddenly remember that on that bus trip to Niamey seventeen years ago Zara had sat next to a little Tuareg girl about her own age. And what they had handed back and forth between them, passing the time, was the birthday doll Zara has forgotten, the one bought in Zinder with the arms and legs rigidly molded to its sides. The one with glossy golden hair springing luxuriantly from its rubber scalp. They had plaited the hair, one taking a turn, then the other, until the doll's head had stood out in braids.

If not Zara, does a young Tuareg woman carry that memory today? And if so, is the doll not lost entirely?

But now we have left behind the vast, open expanse and are following a winding road, are moving meditatively between low hills round as breasts. Or as the crown of the straw hat worn by the Fulani herdsman who raised his hand to us as we passed. Now and then, appearing among the hills, are high flat ledges, mesas, you might call them, a few hundred feet tall, with red laterite soil on top. There are fewer *gawos* now. Instead, we are passing scrubby thorn bushes that dart their prickly branches low, close to the ground. Among them, scattered loosely on the sand, announcing Zinder, are round granite boulders, smooth and still. A camel grazes, head turned away from the taxi. We slowly follow the long loop of the road around a hill and come upon a cluster of huts fenced in with dried millet stalks.

And then, rising in small mounds that give way, around another turn, to higher mounds, the boulders lift from the ground, jostle and roll. As we pass between, they bound higher, lighter, until they are teetering in the air above the hills, granite sides streaming with light. Beloved gates of the city, massive boulders tumbling in the morning sun! Two men have climbed onto the lower reaches of a mound and are sitting in the shade of a giant slab careening above their heads. We leave them behind, and around a hill is another mound hovering against the sky, and then another. At every turn the rocks float buoyant above our heads, still as dawn, defying in their joyful drift the solemn weight of all our griefs, the gravity of sorrow.

But now the clumps of thorn trees are dense, the ground is sand. Here and there, goats wander in the brush. And suddenly, without any warning, the Hotel Amadou Kourandaga appears on the left. In its windows, windows without panes, we can see the soft white of mosquito nets wound above beds already waiting for the night. The hotel vanishes and then, after a little distance, there is a metal billboard: *Buvez Pepsi Cola—Pepsi.*

Everything is from Allah, even the heat, even, around the next broad curve, the Hôpital National of Zinder where people are lying in pain. The woman beside me looks out the window at the offices of the Grandes Endemies, perhaps thinking of her child, perhaps thinking of something else entirely, but in any case we are in town now, riding past the old PTT with the vendors sitting on its steps, down past the high outdoor screen of the defunct Cinema Rex, where on two consecutive nights Mike and I once saw the Russian version of *War and Peace,* and around the corner into the *auto gare.*

Through the hole in the floor, a scrap of yellow sand. The woman leans over, sliding the little boy from her arm onto her back, and covers him with a *pagne.* Then she straightens and knots the ends firmly in front. Someone has swung open the door, so we get out, bending low, stepping carefully. Above us the flag on the fort snaps in the wind, green, white, and orange.

And above that, above the vultures and kites tilting and turning, crossing paths, Job's questions stare from a white ripple of light: *How then can I answer? What words shall I choose?*

When I look down again, the woman and her child are gone. But there, coming forward across the sand, is the one-legged boy with the crutch. He is wearing the gray Bermuda shorts of a month ago and the same shirt with the tiny blue and red flowers. This is his familiar place, the place of travelers, the place where he first stretched his hand to Zara and me. I reach into my black bag and open the wallet, like the bag itself, made in this city seventeen years ago. At one time there was a stamp inside, blue letters going in a circle, *Atelier de Garba: Zinder.* But all trace of that is long gone. From the pouch that holds change I fish out a coin and drop it into his hand. Leaning on his crutch, he looks at me mildly. *Ranki ya da'de,* he says; may you have a long life. Then he pockets the coin in his shorts and swings around to move off and away.

◈   ◈   ◈

The Boissons Fraîches is empty. The fan is spinning overhead but Ahmed and his son are nowhere in sight. I have my pick of the tables and take the one where Zara and I sat a month ago, beneath the fan. In the street, a rooster is crowing, a long piercing cry of jubilation and sorrow. Then there is silence, only the hum of the fan above.

Ahmed's son dips through the strips of plastic, red, blue, and yellow, sticks of French bread bristling from his arms. He disappears in back, but is almost immediately at my side, hand curled to his chest, knocking. Today it is he who is my host, my sponsor, my friend. His eyes bid welcome. Above his head, on the wall, the frosted bottle is still riding the air toward bliss.

A Pepsi, of course. And yes: a plate of *petit pois* and *oignons.*

"Your daughter is not with you today," he says, placing the Pepsi and a glass on the table in front of me.

I shake my head no, she is not with me. We exchange a look, commiserating, solemn.

He lingers a moment, arms crossed. His fingers on his white shirt are long and his wrists are narrow.

"And your father is not here today?" I ask.

"No, today he is in Maradi. He has gone to visit his brother."

But now two men are coming through the doorway, and he turns away, eyes naked, hands open at his sides.

Oh, silence! He needn't have said it, it might have been contained if he had remained silent, but with his words, now, Zara's absence cuts to the quick; becomes a spectacular fact, filling the chair next to mine. An absence sharp around the edges, suddenly, like a vacant tooth, an absence to be indefinitely prolonged by my return to New York. And now—from rejoicing in the bounding rocks—I want only to get out of Zinder and away, away from this place where it is all desire, the ladder reaching for the moon, nothing but that, the hunger for what isn't there: the shadows passing slowly across the veranda, the face one can never see, appearing, disappearing in the same instant, the solitary music heard in the night; last month the yearning for Zara's hand in mine, the child lost forever, and now—just as miserably—the absence of Zara who sat with me then, blue scarf tied in her hair, eating her omelette and *frites*; the grown Zara lost from sight, even then, as we drank our Pepsis, a second time, because she had disappeared into another child, another yet the same, standing on a ledge, in a doorway, who at this hour, while the vultures were landing with a clash on the roof, and the periwinkles were blooming in their ruddy clay pots white in the blaze of noon, had stopped and stared.

Goodbye, my precious girl! Goodbye, my darling!

Second Call to Prayer: *Zuhr*

Into the profound silence of the afternoon breaks the splintering cry from a mosque, announcing the sun is now past the meridian. The shadows have begun their backward sprawl. But after a few steps, stumbling straight up from the Boissons Fraîches, up the road to the hostel where I can wait until Michel's will open later on, retracing our path of a month ago, I am afraid. What am I thinking of, walking around like this, bareheaded in the sun? You could fall down and die of it. Anyone knows that by day the sand holds the heat. Heat that has long ago melted to tepid the block of ice inside the blue plastic canteen wedged alongside Garba's wallet, heat that is turning my face to a flame. A donkey stands flattened against the wall, taking cover in a narrow ribbon of shade. His flanks are bellowing out and in, his tail swishing around his flanks, busy with the flies. Behind him, on a patch of baking wall, a lizard is playing. It flings itself wriggling, then stops, sunstruck.

There is no one out walking, but two men stare at me from under a mat propped on four sticks. One of them is making his ablutions, pouring water from a plastic kettle into his hand, which he then passes over his face and forehead and behind his ears, his lips moving in prayer.

For you, my flesh and my soul thirst—
like the cracked earth, lifeless, without water.

O, let me hear your voice! Let me see your face!
My days are running like evening shadows.
Make haste, for I wither away like grass.

The sand is flowing like a river, and up from the depths,
like a creature rising from the deep, bones clean as a whistle,
sweet as grass. Up, up, and there they are, tossing aside the
sand that streams from their blind and perfect stare. A jumble
of dry sticks, shameless, and, looking out from the sockets, the
gaze of the boy swaying on the scale, gaze washed clean of
shadows, touching each of us in turn.

O cry you mercy!

Far below, below the sand whose heat rises in a quick
light flame, water is running in abundant streams, water clear
and cold. You have only to dig. First remove with a shovel the
loose sand on top. Then raise the mining bar and crack
straight through the ribbon of pale sandstone millennia old.
Lower a bucket; haul it up. Again. Again. Sixty feet down, the
stone will turn dark with moisture. A few more strokes and
water comes bubbling up.

Stored there from the Pleistocene, when dewy grasses
once blew above this ground that would become Zinder. And
before that, before the antelope and quail, an ocean bed where
I am walking, tides rising in tumult high above the earth, tossing huge boulders of granite to a swollen moon.

But not so far below, bones biding their time. First
wrapped in goatskin and carried to the open grave; there
unwound and lifted from the hide. Face, jutting hips and knees,
the penis his hand had sought, all sheltered by shards and bits

of broken gourd from the blanket of sand. "Cause him to enter the Garden, to rest beside quick-running streams."

◆　◆　◆

Behind a concrete block wall, the square pledge of the hostel rides a wave of sand, its glass front door and windows inlaid with pages ripped from magazines. A face, impeccably blank. Just inside the gate, an old man is sitting cross-legged on a mat, his kettle beside him. The dead *gardien* has been replaced, the one who remembered the three little girls. *Ina wuni? Lahiya lau. Ina gajiya? Ba gajiya. To, madalla:* we pass the greetings back and forth, bowing a little, he tapping his chest. But when we come to the end of them, he tells me that for now the hostel has been closed; it will open again someday but he doesn't know when. He looks to see if I have understood, one eye milky, one eye bright.

Around back, the ground slopes downward; but she is no longer there, the woman whose husband died of something in the stomach, whose story made Zara's face go long in sorrow. The hut is empty, dusty gold and burning up, certainly not a place to rest until four o'clock when I will choose a treat for Zara. The hostel is locked, but through the glass door at the back, unpapered, I can see the blunt room we entered a month ago, Pepsi bottles again on the table beneath the fan. I am looking down, eyes averted from the glare, thinking how the donkey stood flush against the wall angling for shade, his tail twitching to one side then the other, when on the blank surface of sand there appears a pair of feet, cracked soles, broken nails, resting in leather sandals.

I look up to see the old man, the living *gardien* who has replaced the dead one, standing beside me.

"*Sai ki zauna,*" he says, why don't I sit down; and indicates the cement wall jutting out from the hostel, a neem throwing shade over one end.

Thirst, already, biting at the back of the throat, like something alive. The blue plastic canteen is shaped like a hip flask, curved to fit neatly in a back pocket, its white plastic top connected by a chain fastened at either end by a hoop. Twisted off, the top jangles alongside the canteen, plastic to plastic. Closing one eye, it is possible to look into the blue depths as into a well: dark water glinting, out of reach. As it had in the *tukunya*, seventeen years ago here in Zinder, the round clay water jars standing on their tripods, brick red sides beaded with sweat, the water inside deliciously cool. Lift the straw circle covers and the water glints silver in the sudden light. Water for lunch, and later on, water after the *sieste*. Water scooped with a dripping ladle. How cool the floors were in the late afternoon beneath bare feet! How they held the promise of night!

Water wet on the tongue, on the back of the throat; but not too much, too soon.

It was El Gouni who said paradise was a garden watered by rivers running beneath. A place of thornless trees and spreading shade—a place to rest until one was summoned into the presence of God. And then a voice, asking if there was anything more one's heart desired.

Oh gently, my mother, my dear. Drop by drop, but cautiously, a little at a time. Each swallow a labor complete. Your mouth eager, alive. Green eyes enormous in their casings of bone, bat eyes, throwing out sudden beams of light. The October sun pooled in the mirror. And in the garden below, away from the shade cast by the tulip tree, chives swept back like hair grown long and unruly, Michaelmas daisies, astors delicate as fleabane, the leaf of sage we had once passed between us, inhaling its scent.

Later, heads pressed together on the pillow, we watched the tangle of shadows on the wall move from mirror to door, the door where I had once stood, a child in tears. And then, because your bones pinned you in place, because the pulse at your temple beat time in your skull, I told you the news: how the yellow leaves of the tulip tree held high and still in the late sun, how the moon would soon leave a path of milky light on the gray slates of the roof. When your hand closed over mine, I waited for my happiness to subside. But it swelled by degrees until, breaking in waves against windows and mirrors and doors, it passed into the afternoon beyond, and I answered that I could want nothing more.

It may be the neem tree throwing shadows on the sand, the supreme consolation of leaves. Or simply the slow drift of the afternoon. At three o'clock the air is charged to the point of combustion, but the steely white light now has something in it of gold. The branches make a shelter, an airy cage of speckled green and winking light. The long shadow of a stork is gliding across the yellow neem berries lying in the dappled sand when the boy with the crutch appears from around the other side of the wall. He passes in front of me and leans, close by, against the corner. When I look at him he smiles. Is there something I should do? In Matameye children are greeted only for lessons in politeness. Besides, there is an air of intimacy in his eyes that makes the formality of greetings seem out of place.

"*Sannu,*" I say.

"*Yauwa,*" he answers, and I remember the little girl swinging between the wooden blocks as we were moving along the street toward the fort, how she had answered Zara in the same way, her smile opening on a missing tooth.

"*Ina yara?*"

He looks at me with interest.

"*Ina yarinya?*" I ask and with a flat hand measure a short distance from the ground.

He looks at me as if there is nothing strange in my question and nothing strange in his not understanding it.

I make fists and plow them toward me, pulling. His eyebrows go up. I repeat my gesture, two, three times, and this time his face lights up in recognition.

"*Kai!*" he says and then, sliding down to join me on the wall, says something I don't understand: I can pick out only two words: *watakila,* which I know means "perhaps," and *tasha,* a word I don't think I've ever heard.

So we sit, our conversation for the moment exhausted, he turning his crutch over and over against his good leg. Sometimes I finger the leather knot on the side of my bag. We are passing the time.

A tiny bright red bird, a Senegalese fire finch, is hopping lightly in the sand a few feet from the wall where we are sitting.

"*Menene?*" I ask, gesturing with my head toward it.

He looks at the bird, looks at me. "*Hausa?*" he asks, and my chin rises sharply in assent.

"*Tsuntsaye,*" he says.

I repeat the word, trying to pronounce it as he does, to slide on the back of the *t* into a sound like "soon."

He watches my mouth and smiles, silent, then resumes swinging his foot back and forth against the wall. After a time his flip-flop falls off and lies upside down on the sand. Holding onto his crutch with one hand, and with the other grasping the wall, he nimbly recovers the flip-flop, turning it over with his toe, then hooking it beneath the thong with his crutch. He looks at me sideways to see if I am watching.

The flip-flop is back on his foot, and I am looking around for some other word I might ask him for, but am distracted by thoughts of Zara, of the day we sat at the door and watched the birds splashing in a puddle left by rain. There had been two female weavers fanning their wings, pale yellow breasts pressed forward until even their beaks were under water.

Then a male weaver joined them, black head glinting, breast the orange of pure gold, a blade of grass in his beak. He lowered the blade to the puddle, turned sharply when one of the females darted toward it. But in a moment he, too, was fluttering and the grass drifted off unnoticed.

At a little distance, a lizard had been watching. At last he began to approach, making frequent stops, up, down, up, down, until he squatted at last, motionless at the edge. Then, orange tail curled behind, he bowed his head and drank. A humble gesture, grateful, profound.

Now and then the boy's aluminum crutch hits against the cement where we are sitting, making a hollow sound. It is topped by a crossbar, designed to fit beneath his arm, and halfway down there is another bar he can hold on to. Not at all like the plain wooden stick a crippled child in Matameye uses to hop about on, shriveled leg wound like ivy round a post. But how did he lose his leg? The end of his stump lines up with the hem of his Bermuda shorts. Was he born that way? A case of infection, of gangrene? A brutal acccident?

He is expertly throwing the crutch back and forth between his open palms, humming a quick staccato beat to himself, glancing over at me from time to time, when another boy comes around the corner of the wall. They begin speaking at once, the way children do, without preliminaries. I can understand nothing, their speech is rapid and abrupt, they could be saying anything at all. Then he turns to me, *Sai an jima*, he says—see you later—picks up his crutch and is gone.

For a few minutes I try to sit on as before, but find that without him I have no taste for it. He kept me company, sat by my side.

Third Call to Prayer: *Asr*

All day I have been thinking that today I would try to remember to do what in Matameye I have so often forgotten: at the third call to prayer observe my shadow in the sand and take note if it is the same length as myself. But when I pass the *gardien* sitting on the mat at the gate and when at the same instant he looks up and I turn to meet his gaze just as the cry breaks shrill in this afternoon air of silence and mourning, there is no longer any question of shadows. The sky has clouded over. He lifts the hand that holds the prayer beads. His milky eye charges me to consider that for now the words the boy has given me, both the one I have asked for and the ones I have not, will serve as my prayer. In his bright eye burns the assurance that Zinder is only another name for Allah.

At the crossroads, the vendors sit barefoot on the wide verandas of the PTT selling their wares: leather boxes, tooled and clasped, the silver four-pointed *croix d'Agadez* on black beaded chains, leather poufs and bags and sandals, brass bracelets for the wrist or ankle, Tuareg swords in tasseled scabbards. Snail fossils found lying about in the sand. From where they sit, the vendors can look across to Michel's *boucherie* and the old Hotel Central. Or they can look across to the sandy stretch between, to the placards sitting squatly on short legs, each with its legend, green letters on a white field:

Sans Auto-Suffisance Alimentaire, Point de Liberté ni Dignité.
En Avant Pour Batir un Niger Nouveau.
L'Authenticité, C'est d'abord le Respect de Soi.
La Justice Sociale Implique la Justice Tout Court.

These are planted on a portion of uncharted ground where the roads running in and out of Zinder intersect. And where, set back a little from the crossroads, the square tower of the fort rises from its mound of tumbling rocks. Behind the fort, across a plateau of scattered boulders and brush, sits the *birni*, fixed long before on Zinder's highest ground, the old walled city with its swallows and minarets and banco houses bolstered by timber, its sand and shadows and heat; the *birni*, enduring source of the city where we draw breath this day, this hour, city even now trembling on the edges of visibility.

The wind that suddenly springs up lifts the dust from the ground and drives it forward at a slant. The fort, at first a dark shape rising against a thickening sky, is swallowed up entirely. Below, on the veranda of the PTT, the vendors are hastily wrapping their leather bags in brown paper. A door bangs shut, then slams back open against a wall. At the cross-roads, as the sand moves forward in sheets, the sign pointing north to Agadez vanishes and reappears. Everything is yellow, the air is yellow, the sky. A Land Rover sweeps past, a dim steady ghost. Then, from out of the dark, the old Hotel Central emerges, now called the Salle de Jeux de Zinder. That's what's written above the picture painted on the wall of a woman playing a guitar. And next to it the sign above Michel's door—*Boucheries Vivres Frais Alimentation, Journaux*—and the looming outdoor screen of the old Cinema Rex.

It is somewhere here we meet. He comes out of the dense yellow fog, a small dark figure leaning on a crutch, bent and determined against the wind. His head is down, his arm crooked over his face. But when we are almost on top of each other, we stop short. I shoot out my hand, palm up. He looks at me, slaps it with his own, then we turn and slap again. For a moment we pause in the swirling dust, guffawing, covering our faces, unsure what to do next. Then we continue on our separate ways. But the palm of each carries the print of the other's. For me, the print of a child's hand in mine, the first in so long, filling its declivities of sorrow.

The first raindrops are making dark spots on the sand when I duck into Michel's. But not before a few have splashed like the touch of heaven on my face and trickled down my back. A wave of cool air sweeps through and suddenly the iron roof is thundering above our heads. There are only one or two people inside the shop. The deaf clerk, who last month told Zara a long story to which she listened with her head held on one side, welcomes me enthusiastically, his mouth going in every direction. "*Ina ruwa?*" he asks, greeting me on the rain. Then, while I am standing vacant, trying to remember the response, he gives it to me. "*Ya yi gyara*": the rains will renew. With his hands he makes expansive gestures, offers to help me to what I need. There are the papers in the rack—*Le Sahel, Sahel Dimanche, Sahel Hebdo*—and there on the shelves the tins of Nescafé and boxes of cornflakes. Bright bars of chocolate, wrapped in colored paper, blue and red.

Above the pounding rain, from the back of the shop where Michel used to slice his meats and cheeses, comes the sound of voices singing, a chorus. Last month Michel was nowhere in sight, but the blackboard was on the wall just as it used to be, the names of items written in script, as they are in Paris, the prices beside them. This time Michel is behind the counter, his butcher's apron tied in back, and I am looking into the first face in Zinder remembered from seventeen years ago. Like mine, altered by the years. His hair is still black and strong, falling across his forehead. But his face is lined, and he seems smaller than I remember, more wiry.

The music is coming from a tape winding in a machine on the counter in back of him. He asks me what I want, his voice rising, like a shopkeeper's in France, at the end of the sentence. I scarcely know. Some Gruyère. That's listed on the board along with the *beurre salé*, the *beurre doux*, and the *yaourt*.

"Pas de gruyère," he says. Then I'll have some Port Salut, Zara will like that. He turns and removes from the shelf behind him a large wheel of cheese and holds the knife above it, measuring. *"De trop?"* he asks. Shaking my head no, not too much, overwhelmed by this man's generosity sustained over so many years, his fear that he might unintentionally charge more than someone wishes, I ask him about the music. What is the singing?

C'est une bande, a tape: *Chansons de la Résistance 1939–1945.* He shows me the little case, the small machine turning on the shelf. He wraps the cheese in paper and hands it to me across the counter. From where I stand I can see through to the little courtyard where once the vultures had kept a sharp eye on the trembling kitten.

"I lived here seventeen years ago," I tell him. "I came to this shop then."

He looks at me politely, nods. "Zinder hasn't changed since that time."

"But no," I protest. "There's the paved road with the street-

lights, the Salle des Jeux next door, the new Hotel Damagaram."

He waves the changes away with his hand. "Niamey has
changed," he says.

"And you," I ask, "do you go back to France sometimes?"

"No," he answers, "not since I left Paris in 1955 to fight in
the *guerre d'Algérie*. I have three children now in Zinder, *des
métisses*."

"You haven't been back in all these years?"

"*Jamais.*"

"And is there no one in Paris?" I ask relentlessly. "*De la
famille, des amis?*"

"*Personne.*"

But now, as if the question has started a train of thought,
as if hunger for a lost place has overtaken him as well, he asks
me if I know the 20th *arrondissement*. Have I been recently to
St. Denis? He grew up on the corner of rue de la Montjoie and
rue des Fillettes, just above a *charcuterie*. The *metro* passed
beneath. Do I know the corner, have I been there? Across the
way there was a kiosk where papers were sold.

A child comes in and stands next to the counter. Michel
reluctantly turns aside from his questions and speaks with her
in very rapid Hausa. I can pick out the word *tasha*. What is
tasha? I ask, remembering how the boy with the crutch had
used the word when I asked about the little girl who had
accompanied him last month, pulling herself through the sand.
"*Tasha,*" he says, but with the dazed look of someone who is
elsewhere, "means *auto gare*."

In the front of the store, I pick out a few things for Zara:
a tin of raspberry jam from Poland, a package of Petits
Beurres biscuits, and three chocolate bars to be kept in the
refrigerator and eaten bite by bite. It is too wet for a baguette.
The deaf clerk, mouthing his approval of my choices, writes

up the list. At the last minute, while he is adding up the figures, I take from the shelf behind me a round box of La Vache
qui Rit. But when he has wrapped everything in brown paper
and tied it neatly with string, the rain still hasn't let up. It
makes a din on the roof. He must not be able to hear, but
standing at the door together, watching the flood swirling on
the sand, we can both see the burning sand has become a pool.
Water is rippling around the legs of the placards, and across
the way the Hotel Damagaram rises from behind what looks
like a waterfall. A car is splashing slowly by, its wheels for a
moment disappearing in a deep puddle. When the clerk opens
his mouth on the word "*Yauwa!*" it occurs to me that by some
stretch of the imagination Zinder awaits me, that I have an
appointment to keep.

Earlier in the day, when I was slogging through the sand
beneath the sun, people sitting under mats and straw roofs
had stared. Now, even though my way is short, one person
after another calls for me to join them. Is it the fear of chill? Of
fever? An old woman looks up from behind the curtain of silver rain streaming off the edges of a thatched roof, her head
to one side, a cupped hand raised inward to her cheek. *Wayyo!*
She waves me toward her, touches the empty place beside her
on the mat. Come, my daughter, sit by me. I imagine joining
her, but instead shout my thanks and move on, confused for a
moment by a vision of green eyes in their casings of bone
reminding me that to pray, after all, is only to choose what is
given. The rain, for instance: so cool, so blessedly cool. Oh, the
relief of it, running down the face, the back, over the arms and
feet. Wherever it touches is absolved of the intolerable blister
of heat that has risen on the skin, hour by hour. Besides, it is
so close where I am going, no distance at all.

And then, in the space of a minute or two, the rain lets up
and stops entirely.

The ramp of sand descending to the *auto gare* is running with water, rivulets crossing and recrossing like those flowing down a beach when a wave drags out to sea. The sand is packed hard. When the water has all drained away, the shallow gulleys will last only until the sand dries from brown to yellow; until it is plowed by the feet and knees and crutches of all who pass here, prints that will soon harbor shadows. At the moment there is no one but myself. The sky, obscured an hour ago by sand, then by rain, is opening to streaks of silver. It is again becoming a place to look into from a distance; like the sand beneath the feet, a map of itself, both a place and a diagram.

Perhaps because of the recent rain, the *gare* is more silent than usual. For the moment there are no beggars chanting, no people shouting to make sure of bundles netted to the tops of vans, no shrieking roosters. Here and there pools of water stand between the waiting taxis. A stork is stepping at the edge of one, then unfurls his wings and lifts into a *gawo* stained dark in places by the rain. The boy, however, is nowhere in sight.

Most of the taxis appear to be empty, but when I inquire for the one going to Matameye, two women standing together talking, *pagnes* pulled over their heads, direct me to a pair of busy vans in the middle of the *gare*. One is pulling out and for a moment I panic. There will not be another returning to Matameye until tomorrow afternoon. But no, that is the one leaving for Agadez. The other is almost filled. In fact there is only one seat left. I pay the driver and quickly climb in. But almost immediately, for no reason I can see, everyone is getting out again. I get out too, but after a minute of standing there, wondering what to do, climb back in. The driver has raised the hood, taken out a spark plug, and is turning it in his fingers. He blows on it, wipes it with a piece of cloth. Then he walks off behind the taxi, disappears from sight.

Through the half-open window I can look up at the fort, now deep orange against a glimmering mackerel sky, and out into the *gare*. Some of the people who have gotten off have vanished, others are talking in groups or have gone over to the fire where a man is roasting *suya*, peppered meat strung on a stick. Fire finches are fluttering around the pools of standing water, dipping and drinking.

It is only when I see him coming down the slope that I realize how sharply disappointed I had been a few moments ago, how I had counted against all odds on finding him here. He is moving quickly, avoiding the puddles with a swift lunge of his crutch. But he must balance and hop, strike and hop again, and for the first time I see—and wonder how I have not seen before—how much easier it would be for him if he had two crutches instead of one. He stops only once, hand extended, when he crosses the path of a man who reaches into capacious white robes and brings out a coin. Then he continues on, passing a little girl with a baby on her back, through the congregation of empty vans, and pauses on the drier patch of sand where the taxi now on its way to Agadez was waiting a few minutes ago. Here he looks around, swings on his crutch in the direction of the window where I am sitting, and leans his head against the pane.

Already the sun has reassembled as a disk. The rocks tumbling in a mound beneath the fort are taking on a silver sheen. Their smooth dark undersides still hold the rain, but huge open surfaces are already glazed with light. The boy and I exchange a look, then he glances down, shifts on his crutch, and stands there, looking out into the *gare*, down at his foot. The aluminum rod of his crutch has sunk deep into the wet sand. It will leave its mark as it has already done on the ramp running with water. The rod holds firm, his arms hang slack.

In the hollow of his neck I can see the throb of his heart. He looks up again and this time we smile, eyes holding after the smiles are gone. I am the first to drop my gaze.

"*Akwai sanyi*," I say, fearful of the silent spaces that are opening around us. It's cool, I mean, the rain has cooled things off. For lack of anything else to say, to do, I untie the string on my package and pass through the window the package of Petits Beurres and one of the chocolate bars. "*An gode Allah*," he says; thanks be to Allah. He puts the chocolate in his pocket but holds on to the Petits Beurres. Then he continues to stand as before, his head against the pane. Now and then we turn to each other, the moment filling our gaze. The skin around his eyes is smooth as glass.

The *gawo* is drying to silver. "*Menene?*" I ask, as a stork glides directly above our heads, long fragile legs thrust stiffly forward, great black wings steady on either side of the white underbelly. Its feet close around the same thorny branch where the first still stands, beak slightly open, beside a nest. "*Shamuwa*," he says, his eyes leaving the stork to rest on mine. His lashes glisten black and thick. "*Shamuwa*," I repeat, putting the accent on the first syllable, as he does, then sliding down to a sound like a hush, a murmur, a lullaby. He beams at me in reply, then repeats the word, pronouncing it more slowly than before. Then we again fall silent, staring through the glass.

The driver of the taxi returns and tinkers again beneath the hood. A man climbs into the taxi behind me, and after him two women. Then the driver comes over and tells the boy to move on, to go someplace else. Hastily, I pass through the window the round wooden box of La Vache qui Rit. He smiles quickly, showing teeth a little stained at the edges with *goro*, deep orange, like the fort, and reaches into the pocket of his shorts. Into my hand he drops the coiled shell of a snail, relic from a time of waters. Then he moves slowly away, holding the cheese and biscuits in his free hand, and when he is near the spot where the man is cooking *suya* over the fire he stops and turns around. A van clatters into the *gare* and sweeps between us, then another. It stalls for a moment, blocking the view. But when the space is clear I can see the little girl swinging between her blocks of wood to where he is leaning on his crutch. When she is sitting in the sand beside him, he drops the Petits Beurres and round box of cheese into her lap. His hand free now, he waves to me and then points down to her, nodding. It was as he said, she is at the *tasha*. I wave back, he waves again, and then we are still, our eyes holding. The girl is resting between her blocks, staring up at him, at me. Once she laughs suddenly, opening her mouth on the missing tooth.

But now the taxi is almost filled; there is a commotion of children being passed from lap to lap, of the old man beside me arranging his robes. A baby cries and is consoled with a breast. Then someone climbs into the front seat, always the last to fill, and the driver swings the doors shut. He climbs into his seat behind the wheel, but when he turns the key the motor sputters and dies. Then he tries again and the taxi lurches into motion. We splash slowly through a puddle and in an instant the fort has swung into closer view and vanished, the rocks floating beneath. The *gawo* sweeps by, the pair of storks immobile in its branches, and then the man turning the *suya* over a bright fire. We are moving toward the road, passing close to the children, and as they flash before the window, already disappearing into the future, I lean out, one hand clutching my shell, the other waving, calling back to them: *sannu, sannu.* The girl waves in return but the boy only looks at me, his eyes washed with light.

NOTES ON
HAUSA ORTHOGRAPHY

Throughout this book, standard Hausa orthography is used except in the following instances:

1. words that have a distinctive pronunciation in Niger dialects (e.g., *koumia*, "shame")

2. proper names
   a) personal names (e.g., Maimoun)
   b) place names (e.g., Kantché)

3. words used on public signs (e.g., *Komai na Allah ne*, "Everything is from Allah")

For the sake of intelligibility, the English marker of plurality, *-s*, is used at the end of Hausa words (e.g., *kwanos*), given that Hausa markers of plurality show considerable variation.

ACKNOWLEDGMENTS

I have been fortunate in the generosity of several people who have provided not only encouragement of every kind during the writing of this book, but have at various stages read the manuscript and made suggestions: Louis Asekoff, Jerome Badanes, Randolph Bates, Mary Ellen Capek, Alfred Corn, Myra Goldberg, Susan Hallgarth, Clifford Hill, Elizabeth Hill, Kathleen G. Hill, Sarah Hill, Margot Livesey, Cassandra Medley, Tom Painter, Carla Roncoli, Diana Trilling, and Jean Valentine.

Margot Livesey's efforts on behalf of this book have been selfless, untiring.

At TriQuarterly Books I am grateful to Reg Gibbons for his kindness.

Grants from the National Endowment for the Arts and the New York Foundation for the Arts have made possible time to write; Yaddo, The Virginia Center for the Arts, and Ragdale have provided the space to do so.

I thank Tom Painter who, while in Niger, traveled to Zinder in order to make sure of points of geography and setting; Hajia Binta Is'mail, for her friendship and conversation; and Clifford Hill, who years ago suggested we go to Africa together.

My sisters, Mary Safrai and Jane Kuniholm, my brother, Bill Balet, and my father, John Balet, have been with me from the begining. My mother, Kathleen G. Balet (1904–1994), remains.

Many others, each glowingly distinct in my catalogue of thanks, have by their warmth and interest sustained the years of writing.

The bare mention of each friend of this book—both named and unnamed—does not suggest the reach of my gratitude.